STATE SANCTIONED

A Special Agent Dylan Kane Thriller

Also by J. Robert Kennedy

James Acton Thrillers

The Protocol
Brass Monkey
Broken Dove
The Templar's Relic
Flags of Sin
The Arab Fall
The Circle of Eight
The Venice Code
Pompeii's Ghosts
Amazon Burning
The Riddle
Blood Relics
Sins of the Titanic
Saint Peter's Soldiers
The Thirteenth Legion
Raging Sun
Wages of Sin
Wrath of the Gods
The Templar's Revenge
The Nazi's Engineer
Atlantis Lost
The Cylon Curse
The Viking Deception

Special Agent Dylan Kane Thrillers

Rogue Operator
Containment Failure
Cold Warriors
Death to America
Black Widow
The Agenda
Retribution
State Sanctioned

Delta Force Unleashed Thrillers

Payback
Infidels
The Lazarus Moment
Kill Chain
Forgotten

Templar Detective Thrillers

The Templar Detective
The Templar Detective and the Parisian Adulteress
The Templar Detective and the Sergeant's Secret
The Templar Detective and the Unholy Exorcist

Detective Shakespeare Mysteries

Depraved Difference
Tick Tock
The Redeemer

Zander Varga, Vampire Detective

The Turned

STATE SANCTIONED

A Special Agent Dylan Kane Thriller

J. ROBERT KENNEDY

ISBN: 9781794686656

First Edition

10 9 8 7 6 5 4 3 2 1

For Jonathan Pitre, The Butterfly Boy, whose indomitable spirit brought joy to those who knew him, and a city to its knees with the news his battle had been lost.

STATE SANCTIONED

A Special Agent Dylan Kane Thriller

"In an ironic sense Karl Marx was right. We are witnessing today a great revolutionary crisis, a crisis where the demands of the economic order are conflicting directly with those of the political order. But the crisis is happening not in the free, non-Marxist West but in the home of Marxism- Leninism, the Soviet Union. It is the Soviet Union that runs against the tide of history by denying human freedom and human dignity to its citizens."

Ronald Reagan, June 8, 1982, Speech to British House of Commons

"Certain people in the United States are driving nails into this structure of our relationship, then cutting off the heads. So the Soviets must use their teeth to pull them out."

Mikhail Gorbachev, Sept. 9, 1985, TIME Magazine

"A Soviet man is waiting in line to purchase vodka from a liquor store, but due to restrictions imposed by Gorbachev, the line is very long. The man loses his composure and screams, 'I can't take this waiting in line anymore, I HATE Gorbachev, I am going to the Kremlin right now, and I am going to kill him!' After 40 minutes, the man returns and elbows his way back to his place in line. The crowd begin to ask if he has succeeded in killing Gorbachev. 'No, I got to the Kremlin all right, but the line to kill Gorbachev was even longer than here!'"

Soviet Era Joke

PREFACE

The Union of Soviet Socialist Republics, the USSR, was founded on December 30, 1922, after a communist-led revolution. For almost seventy years, it dominated the region, and after World War Two, was a constant rival to liberal democracies including the United States and Western Europe.

That all came to a sudden end, when on December 25, 1991, Mikhail Gorbachev resigned as the President of the USSR and declared the office extinct. The next day, the Supreme Soviet voted itself and the Soviet Union out of existence.

The West celebrated, while the long-suffering people of what President Ronald Reagan once called an "evil empire" were subjected to years more of chaos, an economic collapse that rivaled the Great Depression setting in.

And while many in the West feel the collapse of our greatest rival was a good thing in the long term, many today in Russia still yearn for the old days, when the USSR, or the CCCP, was something to be both feared and respected.

And some knew before the collapse, that the reforms being pushed by the last leader of their great nation, Mikhail Gorbachev, would destroy everything they had built.

And they were determined to stop him.

Moscow, Russia

Present Day

"If anything happens to them, it's my fault."

"How do you figure that?" asked Viktor Zorkin, the septuagenarian former KGB agent staring at his companion. "They're half a world away."

CIA Special Agent Dylan Kane couldn't tear his eyes away from the phone gripped in his hand, the speaker blaring bursts of gunfire and static from a frequency jammer as they both listened to what sounded like a vicious assault taking place back home in Langley. He hated feeling helpless, especially when friends were involved, and today he couldn't imagine feeling more so.

For one of those who could die this very minute was the love of his life, the other the girlfriend of the best friend he had ever known.

All because he hadn't thought things through.

"I should have known."

Zorkin grunted. "We all should have known. There was no way she was getting into the US."

Kane frowned, stealing a glance at the old man. "If you're trying to make me feel better, stop."

Zorkin chuckled, patting him on the shoulder. "Sorry."

Kane held up a finger. "Those are MP5s. They must have engaged the targets."

Zorkin leaned closer. "As long as we hear two of those, we're good."

Kane closed his eyes, picturing two of the most important women in his life and what he imagined they would do in a situation he couldn't see, but could only hear.

Then his heart leaped into his throat as the love of his life shouted, "Sherrie, look out!"

And one of the MP5s went silent.

And Kane's head slumped as he knew his best friend's girlfriend had just died.

Red Square

Moscow, Union of Soviet Socialist Republics

May 31, 1988

"It's a beautiful day."

CIA Agent Leif Morrison had to agree with his KGB counterpart. Though neither officially knew the other was a member of their countries' respective clandestine services, they both knew the unacknowledged truth. The CIA dossier on his counterpart's cover was thin, and the file on the real man, Agent Igor Kulick, was equally thin, as likely was the KGB's file on "Secret Service Agent Jeffrey Wainwright." He hated the name, but they weren't about to give a CIA agent's real one to the Soviets, though they too likely knew who he really was, and how green.

I thought we were supposed to be trying to get along?

It was the entire point of this summit between Ronald Reagan and Mikhail Gorbachev. The leaders of the two most powerful nations in the world, sitting down to talk, in the capital of the enemy. Peace was a long ways away, but it was closer than anyone could have thought possible just a few short years ago.

They're terrified of the Star Wars program.

The first time he had seen the video showing the working prototype, he had been stunned. And excited. And a little scared. Though he was young and new to the Agency, he knew how critical the balance of power between the US and USSR was to peace. If the balance were to tip too far in favor of one side, it could trigger a war by the other before it was "too late."

Yet things *were* changing.

The Soviets had reached out, an olive branch extended by their new leader, and the policies of *glasnost* and *perestroika* began to change things. "Openness" and "Reconstruction" were the new way of things here in Moscow, though not everyone supported it. In fact, the hardliners were going apeshit over it, according to his briefing before arriving. The powers that be back in DC and Langley were terrified that an attempt might be made on Reagan, and perhaps even Gorbachev, by his own people.

And he was here to help prevent that, along with a security detail whose numbers he hesitated to guess. He had little doubt it went far beyond the official list, with Washington likely pre-positioning assets in the city for weeks if not months. It was plausible there wasn't a soul in Red Square today actually civilian. Staged clusters of "ordinary" people were hustled into position by handlers for the impromptu stroll about to occur, groups that would allow the two leaders to pretend to interact with ordinary citizens for the cameras. Smiles, handshakes, and baby kissings would be the order of the day.

The baby is probably KGB.

He chuckled.

"Did I say it wrong?"

He turned to his partner, Igor Kulick, his eyes narrowing. "Huh?"

"I said it was a beautiful day, then you laughed."

Morrison smiled, shaking his head. "Sorry, I was lost in thought. I was just thinking about our civilians over there." He gestured toward a collection of a couple dozen, waiting patiently, practicing their smiles.

"And something about them strikes you as funny?"

Morrison shrugged. "I was just wondering if the baby was KGB."

Kulick's eyebrows shot up and he turned to examine the crowd then smiled, shaking his head. "You Americans." He wagged a finger at Morrison. "You are very funny. Always joking." He patted Morrison on the shoulder and they resumed their rounds, on the watch for anything out of the ordinary around the perimeter of today's events. "I can assure you the baby isn't KGB."

Morrison took the bait. "Why?"

"He's smiling."

Morrison snorted. "I didn't think you Russians had a sense of humor."

"Oh, we do, but sometimes you have to be careful what you joke about, and who you joke with."

Morrison regarded him. "I can't imagine living like that."

Kulick shrugged. "Well, if you know no different, it isn't such a big thing."

"Perhaps. Maybe things will change for your country if things go well here."

"Perhaps, though I fear things will get far worse before they get better."

"Let's hope you're wrong."

Kulick's eyes widened slightly and a slight smile broke out. "I did hear a good joke the other day from my cousin."

"Lay it on me."

"Excuse me?"

"It means, 'tell me.'"

Kulick nodded. "Very well, I will lay it on you." He cleared his throat. "Four strangers are assigned to the same room at a hotel. Three of them start drinking and telling inappropriate jokes about the government, and one just wants to sleep. Finally fed up, he sneaks out of the room and goes to the front desk. He orders tea to be delivered to his room in ten minutes, then returns. As the men continue to drink and joke, he walks over to the electrical socket, bends over, and says in a loud voice, 'Comrade Major, I'd like tea sent to my room.' The men stop and stare at him, then a few minutes later, there is a knock at the door and tea is delivered. Everyone drinks their tea in terrified silence, then goes to bed. The man wakes up the next morning and his roommates are gone. He rushes down to the front desk and asks what happened. He's told they were taken by the KGB. 'But what about me?' he asks. 'Oh, you have nothing to worry about. The Comrade Major thought your prank with the tea was quite funny.'"

Morrison slapped a hand over his mouth, struggling to suppress the laugh he couldn't hold back. He gently punched Kulick on the shoulder. "So, you Russians *do* have a sense of humor!"

Kulick grinned. "But don't tell anyone I told you that. It's liable to get me sent to Siberia."

"Another joke?"

Kulick frowned, shaking his head. "Unfortunately, no."

Morrison sighed. "Do your people want freedom?"

Kulick pursed his lips. "Many do, I think perhaps most do, though I doubt many of us truly understand what that means. None of us knows what freedom is. Some of us have seen your movies, but most of those are crime movies to show how violent your country is compared to ours. We hear some of your music, but it is mostly about sex and shirking responsibility. If freedom means a life like what I've seen, I'm not sure I want it."

Morrison grunted. "Don't believe everything you see in the movies. Remember, they're entertainment. They're meant to be an escape from reality. If they always reflected reality, they'd be pretty boring."

Kulick regarded him. "I suppose that's true. Like a good book, it's meant to take you somewhere else, into a world that's more interesting than your own."

"Exactly! Trust me, buddy, you'll love freedom if you ever get it. And once you and your people have had a taste, they won't want to ever give it up."

"I hope you're right, though I'm not confident I'll ever see it. Too many oppose Gorbachev's new ways. It means they could lose their power, and here, power is…" Kulick's voice drifted off as he stared after a man walking past them.

"What is it?"

"Umm, nothing."

Morrison eyed Kulick, the man's face paling slightly, his assigned partner clearly nervous.

No, he's scared.

"What is it? Is it that man?"

"I, umm, can't say."

A pit formed in Morrison's stomach, and the words of the briefing officer echoed in his head. "Report anything out of the ordinary, no matter how trivial."

Does this count?

He wasn't sure. This was his first time in Russia, and his first time on a Presidential security detail. He had been surprised to be assigned. He had impressed his instructors at the Farm, and from all appearances, was on an upward trajectory. His dream was to be an agent, fighting communism in all its forms, whether that meant the Soviets, Chinese, or Cubans. But if the President were to be assassinated on his watch, when he knew something and didn't report it, his career would suffer an early death. "Tell me what's wrong?"

"I…"

Morrison activated his radio. "This is Whiskey-Alpha-Four-Two. We might have a problem here, over." His response was nothing but a burst of static, a burst he had been trained to recognize. "Someone's jamming our frequency." His radio squelched and a voice broke through.

"All stations, report in." Half a dozen all-clears were heard, in order, and when it was his turn, he raised his radio, but before he could respond, he heard his own voice announcing the all-clear. His jaw dropped and he stared at Kulick, who appeared equally shocked.

"What the hell is going on?" He tried his radio again, and again couldn't get through. He turned to Kulick. "What did you see?"

Kulick remained silent, sweat beading on his brow.

"It was that man. You recognized him. Who is he?"

Kulick sucked in a deep breath and squared his shoulders then lowered his voice. "His name is Vasily Boykov. He was removed from his position several months ago."

Morrison's heart hammered. "Why?"

Kulick lowered his voice further. "He spoke out against closer ties to the West."

Morrison's stomach flipped and the blood rushed from his face. "Then there's no way he should be within the secure zone."

Kulick agreed. "No, unless he's been reinstated, but I find that hard to believe."

Morrison shook his head. "No, something's going on here. Our comms are jammed and we've got an ex-KGB agent within the secure zone."

Kulick glanced around nervously. "What do you think is happening?"

"It has to be an assassination attempt."

"Our General Secretary or your President?"

Morrison shrugged. "Does it matter? Either one could lead to war."

Kulick turned a lighter shade of pale. "What do we do?"

Morrison looked about, someone shouting orders as the two leaders were only minutes away from beginning their "impromptu" walk to meet the "average" Russian. "We have to warn our people."

Kulick threw up his hands. "But who do we trust?"

"Is there anyone on your side you can trust?"

Kulick shook his head. "Not really. This is the Soviet Union. You don't really trust anyone. You survive longer that way."

Morrison cursed. "What a way to live."

Kulick glared at him. "And I suppose you trust everyone you work with?"

Morrison regarded him. "Until a few moments ago, yes. But now, I'm not sure. We're all paired up. If someone let him into the zone, then at least one of our people is compromised."

Kulick frowned. "Or dead. I just heard your voice on that radio." His frown deepened. "In fact, how do I know I can trust you?"

Morrison's eyes widened. "We've been together the entire time. If I was in on it, why would I press you on this guy? Why would I try to call it in?"

Kulick sighed. "You're right, of course." He stared at the distinct groups mixed in with security and handlers, "eagerly" anticipating bumping into the two leaders. "We have to do something."

Morrison thought for a moment, wishing to God he had more experience. Then he smiled. "We might not know who to trust, but we know who we can't trust."

Kulick's face brightened. "Boykov!"

"Exactly. We follow him, and see what he's up to."

Kulick's hope faded. "But where did he go?"

Morrison strode with purpose toward the western end of Red Square, Kulick scrambling to keep up. "Well, while you were trying to avoid looking at him, I never took my eyes off him."

"Where'd he go?"

"Down Ilyinka Street."

Kulick sighed. "That's good, then. The leaders aren't supposed to go anywhere near there, and it's closed off at the other end."

Morrison wasn't so reassured. "Yes, but look." He pointed toward the GUM State Department Store. "That would give a sniper a clear view of the entire square, where they're supposed to be walking in the next five minutes."

"But surely they'd be spotted!"

"Perhaps, but by whom? We have no idea how many people are in on it." He quickened his pace.

"I might have been mistaken."

Morrison came to a halt and turned toward Kulick. "I thought you recognized him."

"I did. Or at least I thought I did. Maybe I was mistaken."

"You seemed pretty sure a minute ago."

"I was." He cursed in Russian. "I don't know what to do. This is beyond my level of responsibility. Both of ours. We're supposed to call it in, not investigate."

Frustration at Kulick's indecision had Morrison's chest tightening. "We tried that." He jabbed a finger at the buildings he had seen Boykov disappear between. "Are you coming or not?"

Kulick, trembling, shook his head. "I have to report this."

Morrison growled in frustration. "Then go! Tell everyone you can!"

Kulick shook out a nod then sprinted toward the command post inside the Okhotny Ryad Metro Station at the far end of the square, Morrison resuming his jog to where he feared a sniper was taking up position. If the KGB were involved, that was one thing, but his own people? He would never have believed it if he hadn't heard his own voice come over a frequency reserved for American personnel only. The Soviets had no access to the frequency, at least officially. If they were jamming it, then his people must know, and they'd be taking action.

Yet they weren't.

Nobody was reacting to anything.

Security personnel he recognized were spread throughout Red Square, and none were showing the least bit of concern. It meant either his people didn't know, which he found unlikely, or they were involved in whatever was going on, which he found impossible to believe. Why would anyone on his side of things want to assassinate either of the two leaders? Certainly, they wouldn't want to kill Reagan. He was an incredible President, and was on his way out. If anyone wasn't happy with him, the elections were only months away, and he'd be gone by January.

And Gorbachev? He was the best hope for peace, the best hope for ending the Cold War that had the planet on the brink of nuclear war for decades. If he succeeded in bringing in reforms, the world might finally find the peace it had been seeking for so long.

Why would any American want different?

He reached the street where he had seen Boykov disappear into, and came to a halt, listening for anything out of the ordinary, yet heard nothing. He took one last glance at the carefully staged square, then stepped between the buildings and out of sight. He reached for his weapon and cursed.

He was unarmed.

Only a limited number of American personnel had been approved for carrying, and he wasn't one of them. Only those directly on the President's detail were. His Soviet counterpart was, of course, armed, and was to have provided the firepower should it become necessary. It was one of the reasons given for every American agent having a Soviet double, and one of the reasons given for why the American side of the team had no need to be armed.

Nobody had thought what was happening right here, right now, could happen.

He advanced, his hands raised slightly in anticipation of having to defend himself, his ears straining for any indication someone was about to get the drop on him, but reached the end of the street, finding nothing out of the ordinary, just a physical security barrier blocking anyone from entering the square. Two uniformed Soviet officers stood to his left, another pair to his right, their eyes focused directly ahead. He took one step back, out of their line of sight, not willing to take the risk they'd simply arrest him and sort out later why he was unescorted in the secure zone.

And besides, there was no point in asking them if they had seen anything. If they had witnessed Boykov jump the fence, surely they would have challenged him. If he had attempted to evade capture, there would have been a commotion that would still be ongoing. And if he had papers to let him pass, then he was at least out of the secure zone.

But he didn't believe that was the case. A man scaling a fence this high would be scrutinized, and these men, standing guard, appeared bored and tired. No adrenaline had rushed through their system in the past few minutes, the excitement of someone scaling a fence near their post certain to elicit a reaction.

It all meant that Boykov must still be within the secure zone. He turned, examining the street. There was only one door not barricaded, and it led into the Soviet government's generic department store. It appeared to be a service entrance. He jogged back to it and tried the handle. It was unlocked. He had no idea whether that should be the case, though if he were in charge of security, he would have had it locked, or at least guarded for the duration of the appearance by the leaders of the two most powerful nations in the world.

He pressed his ear to the door and heard nothing. He pushed it open slightly, peering into the darkness on the other side, spotting nothing, though the barrel of a gun could be pointed at his head right now, and his unadjusted eyes wouldn't have seen a thing. Instead, he once again relied on his ears, and once again heard nothing.

He pushed the door open a little wider, sunlight from outside pouring in, and gasped. Two men were down, one with a bullet wound to the head, the other with two to the chest. He reached for his radio then cursed. It was probably still jammed, and if it wasn't, whoever was behind this likely had a radio tuned to the same frequency, and he'd just be tipping them off that he was coming. He pushed the door wider and closed his eyes for a moment, saying a silent prayer for the American agent. He had never met him, but recognized him from the briefings and from training. He was his age, a year behind him at the Farm.

He knelt beside the Russian, patting him down, and smiled as he felt his weapon in a shoulder holster. He pulled the Makarov pistol and checked the magazine, then searched for spares, finding two. He slipped them in his pocket then disabled the safety. A set of stairs were to his left, a long hall ahead with at least a dozen doors and no personnel, the building deemed non-essential and evacuated for the duration of the visit.

It has to be the stairs.

If this was an assassination, then an elevated position would be advantageous. It would reduce the possibility of the shot being cut off by those surrounding the target. He took a tentative step up the stairs and winced as the well-worn tread creaked, yet pressed forward. He was committed now. If there was no one here, then he had nothing to fear, and if there was, they were responsible for the deaths of two agents, and were here to assassinate people under his protection, for reasons unknown.

As he climbed the staircase to the next level, his mind was racing as his heart hammered faster and faster, and he took a beat at the landing to force himself to calm down. Slow, steady breaths, in through the nose and out through the mouth, were repeated several times, and his nerves relaxed if only slightly, though it was already too late to prevent adrenaline from pumping through his system.

He silently cursed at his shaking hands, grasping the weapon with both, trying to steady his aim. He was a crack shot at the Farm. They all were by the end, otherwise they didn't become agents. An agent who couldn't shoot was useless in the field. And the simulations they had put them through were nerve-racking, but in the back of his mind he had always known it wasn't real, and he couldn't get hurt.

Here, today, he would likely die, and it had him on the razor's edge.

He reached the second floor and discovered the door chained with a Soviet security tag hanging off it. He sucked in a deep, slow breath, then hurried up the next flight, discovering another chained door.

One more.

He reached the top and his heart hammered, the blood pounding in his ears at the sight of an unlocked chain. Not cut, but unlocked.

His foe had been provided with the key.

How deep does this go?

He pressed against the wall to the side of the door and listened, but it was useless, his pounding heart overwhelming anything that a calm, experienced agent might have heard.

James Bond wouldn't be shaking.

He frowned.

Yeah, but Timothy Dalton would be quaking in his boots right now.

He smiled.

But maybe not Connery.

He drew another long, slow breath, closing his eyes as he rehearsed what was to come. He would open the door, slowly, listening for any sign of an adversary while scanning from left to right for a target. The building should be empty, and the guards were dead, so anyone he spotted shouldn't be there, and was therefore the enemy.

Shoot first, ask questions later.

He inhaled again through the nose.

Just remember your training, and you'll survive.

He pushed the door open, the hinges giving him away, sending his heart racing once again. He shoved with his shoulder, his weapon held out in front of him, gripped tightly in both hands as he scanned for a target, his arms swinging to his right as he stepped inside and away from the door. Something moved to his right and he dove deeper into the darkened room as the door swung shut behind him. He hit the ground as bullets tore apart the wall where he had been standing, the gunfire muted, his opponent using a suppressor. Rolling, he took aim at the shadows and squeezed off two rounds, the muzzle flashes briefly lighting the room enough for him to see his opponent break to the left and take cover behind a pillar.

He regained his feet and, remaining at a crouch, rushed behind his own pillar nearby. He pressed his back against the cool concrete, his chest heaving, sweat beading on his forehead and racing down his back sending a chill throughout his body.

"Hey, American. Why don't you just leave and let me do my job."

Morrison tried to steady himself, hoping his voice didn't betray the terror that threatened to overwhelm him. "I was just about to say something similar. Surrender now, and I just might let you live." He was impressed with how calm he sounded, at least to himself, then mentally kicked himself for being so bold. "I'm an American Secret Service Agent. Drop your weapon and come out where I can see you."

The man laughed. "You're CIA, Mr. Morrison, and this is the first action you've ever seen, and it will be your last."

Morrison's eyes shot wide.

How could he know that? How could he know my name?

The man's English was good, though it dripped with a Russian accent. He couldn't be sure if it was Boykov, but he took a chance. "And you are Vasily Boykov, former KGB, who may have seen more action than I have, but is a traitor to his country, and *will* die before this day is out."

There was a pause then a chuckle. "I'm impressed, American. You've obviously been well briefed, though I doubt you would have seen my file, or recognized my face. My guess is your double recognized me."

Morrison continued struggling to control his breathing and steady his nerves. If he managed to get a chance for a shot, he had to take it, without hesitation, and couldn't miss because his nerves got the better of him. "You're right. And my partner has gone to get help."

"Help won't be coming, my American friend. Your partner is either already dead, or already in custody. Nobody will be coming to save you."

Morrison's chest tightened. How deep or wide the conspiracy he had stumbled upon went, he had no idea, but it was enough to have provided the man access to this floor with a key, for the radio frequencies to be hijacked, and for Boykov to have gained access to the secure zone despite being terminated from the KGB.

His eyebrows shot up.

You don't get fired from the KGB.

This wasn't America where you could lose your high-security job and reenter civilian life for having expressed a political opinion. This was the Soviet Union. Here, if you expressed an opinion that went against the state, you disappeared. You were either executed or imprisoned. You weren't shown the door. If this man had indeed spoken out against the state, then he should be in a *gulag* in Siberia performing hard labor. But instead, he was roaming the streets of Moscow.

His heart hammered.

He's still with the KGB! They just wanted people to think he wasn't!

And it made sense. How would a junior agent like his partner know what he knew unless the KGB wanted him to know? It was a cover. He shuddered.

That means the KGB, or at least elements of it, are behind this.

Yet none of that explained his frequency being commandeered, with his own voice recorded and played over the radio waves. Elements of the CIA or Secret Service had to be in on it as well. Either here, on the ground, or back stateside. They obviously had their files. All their files, if Boykov recognized a lowly agent like himself.

No, there's no way he'd remember me. My face, perhaps, but not my name.

And how did he know who he was? It was too dark in here.

He's not working alone. They watched you come in!

His heart hammered.

More could be coming!

Something pressed against the back of his head and he cursed, his shoulders sagging. He held up his right hand with the gun, and it was removed by the second man it had taken him too long to figure out might be coming. He raised both hands, stepping from behind the pillar providing him with cover from Boykov, but also a blind spot this second opponent could use. He looked down at the man's feet.

Socks.

He shook his head. "Good thinking."

The man glanced at his feet. "I thought so." The man's English was perfect. If he didn't know better, he'd have thought this man was as American as he was. He said something in Russian to Boykov.

I have to learn Russian.

Boykov stepped out from behind the pillar, the faint light coming in from around the drawn blinds of the windows lining the wall behind Morrison, revealing enough of his details to confirm it was indeed Boykov. "It's about time." He checked his watch. "They'll be here any second." He rushed to the window and opened a rifle case that had gone unnoticed sitting on a table. A sniper rifle was quickly assembled then positioned. Boykov lifted the blind slightly, perhaps two inches, enough to give him a shot apparently, though not enough for anyone monitoring the windows to notice.

The second man walked toward Boykov, keeping his weapon trained on Morrison. "Do you have the shot?"

"Yes, I see the bastard."

"What color is his suit?"

Boykov kept his eye pressed against the scope. "Powder blue. His blood should show quite nicely for the cameras."

"So, the target is Gorbachev. You crazy sons of bitches."

It was a curious statement. Curious enough to break Boykov's concentration as he turned to look at his partner. "What kind of—"

But his question was cut off as the man pumped two rounds into Boykov's back.

Morrison's mouth was agape as the man turned back toward him, unscrewing his suppressor, Boykov's final moments still playing out behind his savior.

"You okay, kid?"

Morrison said nothing, still in shock. The man grabbed him by the shoulder and gave him a shake.

"Kid, you okay?"

Morrison nodded. "Wh-what just happened?"

"Nothing. You're going to go outside, find your partner, tell him you found nothing, and it must have all been a false alarm. If anyone asks you anything, you just heard your voice over the radio, and the frequencies were jammed when you tried to call in a concern. I was never here, and you were *definitely* never up here."

"But, I, umm." Morrison stopped then stared at the man. "Who are you?"

"I'm a ghost. Now get out of here, and forget everything you saw."

Minkin Holdings Headquarters

Moscow, Russia

Present day, four weeks before the assault

Natasha Ivashin stared at the man sitting behind the large antique desk, the hand-carved creation a masterpiece worth more than she could possibly imagine. She hadn't exactly grown up poor, though she would have been unimaginably so if it weren't for her Uncle Cheslav. Yet he wasn't her uncle. Not really. He was a family friend, her father's best friend apparently, who had taken care of her and her mother after her father's death decades ago.

Almost thirty years ago.

She had few memories of her father, though the last was by far the worst. She had found his body, slumped behind a desk far humbler than this one. She had only been five. The memories of that day, and those that followed, were a jumble now, mostly created by her mind from stories she told herself.

But the image of her father, the gun he had used to take his own life still gripped in his hand, would never leave her. It was an image that haunted her dreams, an image that would never allow her peace.

An image that had ruined her life.

She had few happy memories, despite making a success of herself. Uncle Cheslav had made sure they were fed and clothed, and had a roof over their heads. He had paid for her education, and had been the father figure she needed, even if his appearances were rare. He was now a senior minister in the Russian government, recently elected, and a staunch supporter of the President. He was a self-made man, worth millions if not tens of millions, and his time was precious.

Far too precious for the likes of her.

Yet he had made time for her after her mother's death several weeks ago.

Though it had seemed reluctantly.

"I know why you're here."

It had taken her aback. "So, you knew all this time?"

Uncle Cheslav nodded. "I did. Not to speak ill of the dead, but I didn't agree with your mother hiding the truth from you for so long. Obviously, you were too young to be told when it happened, but I felt after you turned eighteen, you should have been told. Your mother, God bless her, disagreed, and I respected her wishes."

Natasha dropped into a chair across from her uncle. "What can you tell me?"

"What do you know?"

She waved the letter that her father had left her thirty years ago, only now opened. "He said he was involved in something shameful, and took his life to protect us from what he feared might come."

"And that's all?"

"Yes. On her death bed, mother gave me this, and told me you could answer any questions I might have."

Cheslav drew a breath, steeling himself for what was to come. "Ask me anything."

"What was he involved in?"

Her uncle frowned, exhaling loudly. "Very well. I will tell you, but you must never repeat it to anyone, understood?"

She leaned forward eagerly. "Yes."

"Your father was part of a plot to assassinate Mikhail Gorbachev."

Her jaw dropped as her eyes widened. She fell back in her chair, her head slowly shaking at the revelation. "It…it can't be!"

"I'm afraid it is, my dear."

"But why? I mean, is it true?"

Cheslav's frown deepened. "I'm afraid so. But don't blame your father. Those were different times. Many of us feared what would happen should Gorbachev's reforms be allowed to continue, and in some ways our concerns were borne out. The Soviet Union that we all loved and served collapsed, and near anarchy ensued. It's taken almost thirty years for us to recover, and many feel we still have far to go."

She stared at him in silence before finally gathering the strength to continue. "Do *you* believe that?"

He sighed. "I do, to a point. That's why I ran for office. To try and help the country I love."

"And father? He obviously failed. What happened?"

"I don't know everything, as I wasn't involved in the plot, but after the collapse, he told me as much as he dared, for he feared if anyone knew I had been told, my life would be at risk." He sighed, shaking his head. "Your father was a good man, my dear, the best. He was my best friend from childhood, and we served together with honor in the KGB for decades. Yet all that loyalty and service was wiped from the record when your father failed in a mission that I'm convinced he hadn't conceived, merely executed on orders from above."

"Who? Who gave him the orders?"

Cheslav shook his head. "I have no idea, and your father never said. But when he failed, no one could obviously come out and say why he was disavowed, but he was. The Soviet Union collapsed three years later, the KGB was rebranded, and spies like your father and me were retired. I with honor, your father in disgrace. The worst part, though, was that he was to blame, and he feared that those who had given him the orders would seek their revenge. And in those days, it was family they took it out on first."

She stared at him, aghast. "Me and mother."

"Exactly. So, he took his own life to protect the two of you from what might come."

Her voice cracked. "Would they have come for him?"

He nodded. "I'm afraid so. Many died in those days, silently, off the radar. Much of it was made to look like gang violence, but we knew what was really going on. It was payback time, and your father was most likely on someone's list. As were you and your mother. The fact you were both allowed to live, with nothing interfering in your success, shows your father's sacrifice was worth it, don't you think?"

Tears rolled down her cheeks as she pictured him dead in his chair, a gaping hole in his head. "Never," she whispered. She looked up at her uncle, her eyes blurred with tears. "I would give my life this instant if it meant just another day with him."

Cheslav closed his eyes for a moment, his shoulders shaking as he struggled for control. He finally opened them, revealing his own pain. "As would I, my dear, as would I. But there is nothing we can do to change the past."

Her hands gripped the arms of the chair, squeezing tighter and tighter as her heart hammered with a rage that shocked even her. She had always been prone to fits of anger, of tantrums so violent she had terrorized her mother when she was younger. It was kickboxing, a sport her uncle had suggested, that had allowed her to control her untamed aggression. Yet beating the living shit out of inanimate objects, or sparring with rules that protected the safety of her opponent, hadn't been enough.

Enter mixed martial arts.

She had embraced it, and become quite good, though those years were behind her. She was a respected educator now, teaching mathematics at a local high school, where kicking ass in public was frowned upon.

Yet she didn't need the outlet anymore. She had grown out of it, the fits of rage a thing of the past.

Until now.

She sprung from her chair. "I need to know who is responsible."

Cheslav shook his head, but not before recoiling from the rage. "I-I told you, I don't know."

"Was my father the one who was supposed to pull the trigger?"

Cheslav shook his head. "No."

"Then who was?"

"There was one trigger man, though there were several others involved in the mission, according to your father."

"So, they're the ones who failed."

Cheslav composed himself and pointed at the chair. She sat. "Yes, they were the ones that failed, but your father was in charge, so bore the blame."

"But if they had succeeded, then there'd be nothing to blame my father for, and he'd be alive today."

Cheslav shook his head. "No, we don't know that. There could have been a world war if he had succeeded. There were Americans involved as well. They were going to make it look like the Americans did it, to prolong the Cold War. Countless millions could have died if that conflict had continued, and tens of millions if not billions could have died if there had been war." He leaned forward. "No, my dear, I thank God every day that he failed. Anything is better than war."

"That may be true, but I want names. I want them to pay like my father did."

Cheslav sighed heavily. "And how are you going to make them pay?"

"I'm going to kill every last one of them. And you're going to help me."

She had left the room, returning to her empty home she had shared with her mother. She had hoped her rage would subside, as she was certain her uncle had hoped as well, but it had grown into a white-hot inferno only blood could quench.

And her uncle had come through, as he always did.

"If we are to do this, then it must be done properly, and swiftly."

She had embraced him the moment the words were delivered in her doorway, then the shocking revelation that he had lied to her was revealed the moment they sat—her father had given her uncle the names of several involved, and a copy of the report naming the two responsible for foiling the attack.

Her rage grew.

And the plotting began.

Her uncle provided files on the targets, and devised their methods of execution, all with the aim of drawing out into the open those who might ultimately be responsible.

For Cheslav feared it went to the core leadership of the country, and they'd be nearly impossible to reach.

But the plan was solid, though more complicated than she had hoped.

Yet its complexity did make sense when explained to her by her uncle, who had far more experience in these things than she did.

And that was why she was sitting here today, meeting with a man involved in the plot that had ultimately taken her father's life, resisting the urge to kill him where he sat.

For he had something she needed.

He pushed a small box across his desk. "I've been instructed to give you this."

She glanced at it, but didn't touch it. "You must owe my uncle a great deal to heed his request."

The man frowned. "Let's just say your uncle is a very powerful man, and men like me aren't in any position to deny men like that anything."

She grunted. "You're one of the richest men in Russia. I doubt there's much he can do to touch you."

The man chuckled. "How naïve you are, little one." Rage flared in her gut at the disrespect. "Men like me are nothing without men like your uncle behind us. Yes, we have more money than we know what to do with, but with the snap of our President's fingers, we can be tossed in prison on falsified charges, everything taken from us." He shook his head. "No, little one, I had no choice but to heed your uncle's demands." He pointed at the case. "I don't know what you're going to do with that, but I'll warn you, it is *extremely* dangerous. If you're not careful, you *will* die." He leaned closer. "And if you're caught, you will *absolutely* die." He indicated the case again. "Treachery like this never goes unpunished."

She rose, taking the case. "When my job is finished, I don't care if I live or die." She tucked it into an inner pocket of her jacket, wishing she had a gun. She eyed a letter opener sitting on the desk.

That will do.

"And what exactly is this job?"

She stepped closer, leaning forward, her balled fists pressed against the top of the antique masterpiece. "To kill everyone involved in the assassination attempt on Gorbachev in 1988."

The man's eyes flared and his jaw dropped as she grabbed the letter opener, tossing the sheath aside. "Starting with you, Yury Minkin, the man who gave the briefing."

An alarm sounded and she glanced over her shoulder as the door to the office opened. The busty blond secretary that had shown her in earlier rushed through the door, about to say something, when she gasped.

And it was all the distraction Minkin had needed.

Natasha felt an iron grip on her hand, her wrist bent at an ungodly angle, the letter opener clattering onto the desktop as she dropped to her knees.

"What's going on?"

"Yury, we're being raided!"

The grip on her hand was broken instantly and she cradled it against her chest as she was forgotten.

"What are you talking about?"

"It's the police! They're in the lobby and on their way up!"

Footsteps pounding in the hallway neared and Minkin paled. He pointed at Natasha's pocket containing the case. "If they catch you here with that, we're both dead."

He turned to his secretary. "Lock the outer doors and go to lunch. Don't come back until you hear from me."

She just stood there, frozen.

"Do it! Now!"

She yelped and jumped, then disappeared, closing the door behind her. Minkin locked it then beckoned Natasha over to the wall, left of his desk. He pressed on the corner of a panel and there was a click, the panel sliding aside a moment later. He pressed a button on a keypad, doors parting to reveal a private elevator. He shoved her inside. "This will take you to the basement. Follow the hallway to the end. There's a door that leads to the street on the next block."

She stared at him. "Why are you helping me? I just tried to kill you."

"Because what I procured for you and your uncle means treason, and they'll hang me for sure. Your personal business with me is something entirely different, and one day we'll discuss it like civilized individuals, and perhaps you'll let me live." He reached inside and pressed a button then stepped back. "Good luck, little one. I hope we meet again so I can explain why you're so wrong."

Zizzi Restaurant

Salisbury, United Kingdom

Three weeks later

"It's a beautiful day."

Igor Kulick smiled at his daughter, Anna, visiting for the first time in two months, despite only living on the other side of the city. Yet notwithstanding her infrequent visits, he was still thankful. His wife had long passed, and Anna was all he now had.

And who's to blame for that?

It was his own fault, his loneliness. He had made the choices he had, and because of it, had fled his homeland. Though was it his fault? What had happened in Red Square all those decades ago hadn't been his fault, though his attempt to report what he knew had killed his career. He had never seen the American he had been partnered with again, though assumed he had succeeded in foiling Boykov's assassination attempt, as both leaders had survived their staged stroll unscathed.

Though as his supervisors had insisted, there had been no assassination attempt. It was all in his head. He had never seen Boykov, and he had abandoned his post, leaving an American spy unescorted, a spy who had spent perhaps hours stealing state secrets.

Despite all their assurances to the contrary, something *had* happened, he was certain. While the official story had been that nothing untoward had occurred, the rumor mill was rife with reports of several shots being heard, and activity at one of the buildings lining Red Square.

And then there was Dimitri Golov.

He wasn't seen again, and Kulick knew he had been assigned to one of the two buildings Boykov had disappeared between. His disappearance could mean only one of two things. That he had been killed, perhaps by Boykov, or he had been "disappeared" for failing in his duty, or for interfering in whatever Boykov had been up to.

If Boykov had indeed been there, which he had never doubted despite his contrarian statements expressed to the American, then he shouldn't have been. The fact he was, told him more than one was involved, and that likely meant someone on the Russian side. And he had had over thirty years to think about that day.

How had he known about Boykov? Boykov was a senior agent, Kulick only a junior. How did they all know about him? How did they know why he had been terminated? And if he had been, why hadn't he been executed or sent to Siberia? Things back then worked differently, though not as differently as many in the West liked to think. The apologists on the left and in the media when it came to the current

Russian leadership were delusional if they thought Russia was a democracy. Yes, it had flirted with the notion for several years, but now the elections were merely for show so that the great leader could claim legitimacy on the world stage. If the man had his way, he'd name himself supreme leader, abolish elections, and rid himself of the *Duma* and the Federation Council.

Welcome to the new Russia, same as the old.

Just with an opponent more naïve than the previous.

"You're somewhere else again."

He flinched at his daughter's voice, then smiled. "I'm sorry, Anna, what did you say?"

"I said it was a beautiful day."

He sighed, staring out the window of the restaurant, their late lunch cleared away only moments before. "It is, isn't it?"

"You're thinking of home again, aren't you?"

He chuckled. "You know me so well."

"Why won't you tell me what has you so troubled?"

He frowned. He had kept his secret, kept it for over thirty years. His career had been ruined, and when the Soviet Union collapsed shortly after, he had resigned and become a police officer, only later joining the FSB, the replacement to the KGB, hoping things had changed and he might help his new country prosper.

And for a while, things did improve, though not before descending into near chaos. Even under the new leader, things had improved, though once the iron grip was established, the old ways started to return.

And he had spoken out against them, tried to warn others of what was happening, tried to remind those who had been through it, and educate those who hadn't, what they risked returning to should things go unchecked.

And he had been given a beating the likes of which he would never forget, his poorly set clavicle reminding him every time he put on a jacket.

He had used his contacts to get into Poland the very next day with his wife and daughter, and eventually made it to England, eventually gaining his British citizenship.

"Just thinking of your grandparents."

"I wish I had met them."

"So do I."

And you still could, if you had only kept your mouth shut.

His parents were still alive, though they had no idea he still was. For their own safety, he had never contacted them in the almost fifteen years of self-imposed exile.

And it killed him inside a little more each day.

"They were wonderful people, but life is hard back home, and they died too young." He patted her hand then placed several bills on the table to pay for their lunch. "Not like here. You'll live to a ripe old age, I'm sure."

She rose, grabbing her jacket from the back of her chair. "So will you, Father."

He smiled. "Let's hope so."

They stepped out onto the street and he drew in a slow breath. "It *is* a beautiful day."

"So, you did hear me."

He smiled. "I always hear, Anna, though sometimes it takes a while for me to actually listen."

She growled. "Men!"

He chuckled. "And speaking of men, how is Michael?"

Her eyes widened. "How do you know about him?"

"A father knows."

"Uh huh." She eyed him for a moment. "Sometimes I wonder if you weren't a spy in your former life."

He tensed for a moment, then held his silence a little bit longer.

"See, I think I'm on to something."

"What makes you say that?"

"You hesitated."

He shrugged. "Then I guess I wouldn't have made a good spy, now, would I?"

She laughed. "My father the spy! What a notion!" She took his arm and rested her head on his shoulder. "I miss Mom on days like these."

His eyes burned and his chest heaved a single time. His daughter noticed and patted his arm as he whispered, his voice cracking, "I miss her every day."

It had been a car accident. A drunk driver. Hit and run. The murderer, for that's what he or she was for getting behind the wheel of a two-ton killing machine, had never been caught. If he were a more suspicious soul, he might have thought it was a message from his former employers that he had been found, and that if he caused any more problems, his daughter might be next.

But accidents happened.

Drunks got behind the wheel.

And they too often got away with it.

Whoever had done it was lucky. If Kulick knew who it was, they never would have seen the inside of a courtroom. They'd have died a long, horribly painful death before given a chance at formal justice.

"Now you've got me crying."

He smiled down at his daughter as she removed her gloves and wiped her tears away with the side of her finger. "I'm sorry."

"Never apologize for missing Mom."

He put an arm around her and squeezed. "She's with me every time I see you. You look so much like her, it's uncanny sometimes."

Anna put her gloves in her pockets and sniffed. "I know, I know, I'll try to see you more often."

He laughed. "I thought I was being subtle."

"Yeah, like a hammer."

He opened the gate to his humble home, holding it open for a woman who mumbled a thanks as she left the neighbor's to his left, his home just one of a long row of attached houses in the tenement. He closed the gate behind them, climbing the few steps to the front door.

He unlocked it and pushed it aside, letting his daughter pass. She stepped inside and he followed, catching the toe of his shoe on the threshold, stumbling forward. She reached out for the door with one hand, for him with the other, and he cursed for the umpteenth time at the strip of wood that had caused him so many problems over the years. "I think it's time I give up on the landlord fixing that, and just do it myself."

Anna stepped forward and knelt, one hand on the knob, holding the solid door open, as she examined the guilty party. "Wouldn't you just need to sand it down a few millimeters?"

He shrugged. "I was never a handyman, but I think so."

She pointed. "Just remove the two screws at either end and I can take it home with me. Michael, as I have a feeling you already know, is a carpenter. He can fix it." She closed the door then pulled her shoes off, following him into the sitting area.

"Or, you could bring him over here, and I can meet the young man."

She blushed. "Fine, Father, I'll bring him over."

"Good, then that's settled." He set about making tea, a habit he had picked up upon arriving in his new country, and one he honestly enjoyed, when he gasped, his entire body spasming.

His daughter rose from her chair, concerned. "What's wrong?"

He took a deep breath, trying to calm his hammering heart, then shook his head. "I don't know. Just a wave of—" Every muscle in his body contracted at once, his fingers twisting unnaturally, his arms drawn up toward his face at the elbows before he collapsed.

"Oh my God!" His daughter rushed around the counter and dropped to her knees beside him as he continued to shake uncontrollably, jolts of pain randomly shocking different parts of his body as he gasped for air, his breaths becoming shorter and shallower as his hammering heart slowed. He stared up into his daughter's terrified eyes, trying to speak, trying to say goodbye, yet nothing but a strained sigh escaped.

Anna leaped to her feet, grabbed the phone off the wall, and dialed 9-9-9. Suddenly she cried out, dropping to her knees then to the floor beside her father, the emergency operator's voice a fading sound in the distance as Kulick slowly lost his battle to survive, destroyed inside at the knowledge his daughter would die with him, all because of a past she knew nothing about.

For he knew who had done this to them.

And that they would never pay.

Morrison Residence

River Oaks Drive, McLean, Virginia

Leif Morrison leaned back in his chair, his eyes burning from another long day at the office. His wife was visiting her sister for the week, and with the kids no longer living at home, he was alone in an empty nest.

Save the security detail surrounding his property.

As the CIA's National Clandestine Service Chief, he was a high-priority target, and was protected appropriately, though as he knew from operations he had authorized over the years, any security could be penetrated if the opponent was determined enough. One just hoped one's own security was enough to delay any foes from succeeding before backup arrived.

Dylan got in no problem.

He grunted at the thought of one of his top agents as he sipped his eighteen-year-old Macallan. He had a stable of agents that he could rely upon to do the job and do it well, but Dylan Kane was the best of the best.

They should be making movies about him.

Not only was Kane a skilled operator, he was also fiercely loyal, not only to his country, but to his friends, and though Morrison was his boss, he liked to think that he might be included among those numbers, even if only on the periphery. Kane had few friends, though perhaps more than most in the spy business. Yet they were all in the business themselves. It was a tight crew that Morrison never doubted he could rely on for the most difficult, and the most delicate, of missions.

He sighed, two televisions playing CNN and Fox News, trying to find a balance in the reporting, yet finding none. The news networks had become nearly useless over the past few years, dominated by one-sided opinion. They were all guilty of it, and he frankly had no idea how to solve the problem as long as no side recognized it. He only watched them now in case something major was happening in the world, and even then, they were merely background noise, usually on mute or a very low volume. In his line of work, he typically knew what was happening long before the press did, and far before the masses.

His phone rang, his private line, and his eyebrows rose at the number shown, a display quickly back-tracing the call to Salisbury, United Kingdom. A hospital.

Odd.

He answered, and a hesitant voice replied. "Umm, hello, who, umm, am I speaking to?"

Morrison's eyebrows rose slightly at the woman's voice. "You called me, ma'am. How about you start?"

"Yes, umm, of course. I'm sorry to disturb you, but this is a rather, umm, odd situation."

Morrison set his scotch aside, positioning a pad of paper on his lap and retrieving a pen from a beer stein sitting on the end table, the vessel purchased on a family vacation to Munich too many years ago. "Why don't you tell me what's going on?"

"Yes, of course. My name is Midge Aldrin. I'm a nurse at Salisbury District Hospital. We had two patients brought in a short while ago, both in critical condition and now in comas. I was going through their personal effects to find any family they might have, and found a curious note in the man's wallet with this number written on it."

She had his full attention now, his heart rate rapidly increasing as he scribbled notes. "What did it say?"

"It says, and I quote, 'If something odd should happen, call this number, and tell him Whiskey-Alpha-Four-One needs help from Whiskey-Alpha-Four-Two.'"

Morrison drew a quick breath and held it as a flood of memories threatened to overwhelm him. Moscow. 1988. It was something he hadn't thought about in years, though they were memories he'd never forget. Like his callsign, and that of his Soviet counterpart, Igor Kulick, whom he had never seen again. "Does it say anything else?"

"No, just that."

"Have you told anyone?"

"Not yet." There was a pause. "Why? Shouldn't I?"

Morrison didn't respond. "Tell me what happened to him."

"He and his daughter were brought in. Some kind of poisoning."

Morrison tensed. "Tell no one you called me, and keep the note on your person. Someone will contact you shortly. And, ma'am?"

"Yes?"

"Tell your people to look into Russian nerve agents."

"Wh-what?"

She sounded terrified.

As she should.

"Tell your people now. All of your lives may depend on it."

Kane/Fang Residence, Fairfax Towers

Falls Church, Virginia

Dylan Kane collapsed on top of his partner, completely spent, completely satisfied, and completely in love. Lee Fang was everything he could have asked for in a woman, and more. She was the only woman he had ever loved, the only woman he didn't have to lie to about what he did for a living, and the only woman he was fairly certain would have a good chance of kicking his ass.

"I love feeling you on top of me. It makes me feel safe."

He propped up on his elbows and smiled down at her, her cheeks flushed, sweat drenching both their bodies. "Coming from you, that means a lot."

"I love you."

His smile broadened. "I love you too." He leaned in and kissed her gently, then with a passion that threatened to signal the beginning of round four, their lovemaking having begun almost the moment he had crossed the threshold, returning from a three-week mission in Asia, the least exotic stop, Hong Kong.

She was lonely here, and he hated that fact, though moving into the same building where his best friend lived with his girlfriend, both CIA, did help. They knew her back story, and they knew she was living in exile from a Chinese government she had betrayed to save it from rogue generals attempting to trigger a coup in America. It meant an isolated existence. She couldn't work, she lived off a generous stipend provided by a grateful America, and kept busy staying fit, learning about her new country, and making him feel like the luckiest man alive. He had extracted her from China, then fallen in love, as they both recognized themselves in each other.

It had been fate.

"We're supposed to have dinner with Chris and Sherrie in less than thirty minutes."

Kane grinned. "I can do thirty."

"But we both have to shower and get dressed."

Her gasps between each word told him she was seriously considering canceling their dinner plans. "Let's save time and change the venue." He climbed off her, somebody wagging hello, and grabbed her svelte, short frame, slinging her over his shoulder as he walked her caveman-style into the bathroom, her giggles and playful slaps of his ass signaling her consent with the manhandling. He lowered her onto the counter and she grabbed onto him, wrapping her legs around his waist, and he gasped as they once again became one.

"Shower!" she cried as their passion grew, and he carried her over to the shower stall, pulling open the door and stepping inside, their bodies still entangled, then pushed her against the wall. She grasped for the tap, spinning it, and they both gasped at the ice-cold water that drenched them for the first few moments before it finally reached the temperature they were already at.

His watch pulsed a coded signal into his skin, a signal only he could detect from the CIA modified Tag Heuer.

He cursed.

"What?"

"My watch."

"Don't…you…dare…" She cried out and he gave into his own desires, setting duty aside if only for a few more moments. Spent again, she slid down his body then stared up at him, slapping his cheek gently. "You may go now."

He chuckled. "Sometimes I think I'm just a piece of meat to you."

"I wonder if that's why they call it 'porking?'"

Kane snorted. "Where did you hear that?"

She shrugged as she lathered up. "Some old comedy on Netflix."

"Well, let's not share that one in polite company." He activated his watch and his eyebrows shot up at the message scrolling across the display.

"What does it say?

"Umm, don't be late for dinner."

She paused her ablutions. "Huh?"

He reread it. "It says, 'Don't be late for dinner.'" He looked up at her. "What do you think that means?"

She resumed washing her incredibly fit body. "I'm guessing Chris is playing a trick on you."

He grunted. "More likely Sherrie. Chris knows better."

Chris Leroux was his best friend from high school, and after discovering they both worked for the CIA, their friendship had been rekindled, and they were as close as they had ever been. In fact, Leroux was one of the few people in this world he trusted, besides, of course, Fang and Leroux's partner Sherrie White, a fellow CIA Agent.

And, of course, his old buddies from his stint in Delta.

Leroux was an Analyst Supervisor, an accomplishment for someone so young, but his skills were second to none, and Director Morrison had given him a chance with his own team. It had worked out brilliantly—once the painfully shy guy had gained some confidence and learned how to be a boss rather than just the guy receiving orders.

He was his best friend, and they were due for dinner in only minutes.

But Leroux would never abuse the CIA's communications infrastructure for a joke message.

Though he might use Kane's own private network.

Over the years, as a self-preservation measure, Kane had set up a series of secure servers around the world, known only to himself, in case he was disavowed for some reason, or something were to happen to his country's ability to communicate with him. This backup network assured communications with those he trusted, and a rare few knew how to send him discrete messages, those then relayed to his watch or other select devices.

And it was something he couldn't see Leroux abusing.

But Sherrie…

She was a joker, and did have access, yet again, he doubted it.

He stepped back into the shower.

"No hanky-panky."

He nodded. "No time." He quickly showered as Fang stepped out, toweling off. She eyed him.

"That message has you concerned."

"What makes you say that?"

"You haven't looked at me since you got it."

He paused for a moment, making a point of ogling her. "Better?"

She snapped the towel at him. "A little." She headed for the bedroom. "You don't think Chris or Sherrie sent it, do you?"

He shut the water off and began to dry himself. "No, I don't."

"Then who?"

He quickly towel-dried his hair. "No idea, but the list is very short."

"Who else knew we had dinner plans?"

He stepped over to the vanity and grabbed the antiperspirant. "That's just it. Besides us, Chris, and Sherrie, I can't think of anyone."

Fang reentered, sporting a bra and panties, going to work on her hair.

"Going for the wet look?"

She frowned at him. "No time to dry my hair now, thanks to you."

"I think someone else can share in the blame."

She reached down and squeezed Kane Jr. "He rarely gets a say in the matter."

He chuckled. "Don't start something we don't have time to finish."

Her hand jerked away. "You're insatiable."

He placed a kiss between her shoulder blades. "Only for you, babe, only for you." He headed for the bedroom and quickly dressed, returning to join Fang in their shared bathroom, finishing up then admiring himself in the mirror. "How do I look?"

"Like a very satisfied man."

He gave the mirror a toothy smile. "I *am* gorgeous, aren't I?"

Fang struck a pose beside him. "A gorgeous couple?"

He nodded. "Yup. I'm gorgeous, and you make us a couple."

She swatted him, a feigned hurt expression reflected in the mirror. "Careful, I might just cut you off."

"Why punish yourself?"

She swatted him harder. "Don't make me hurt you."

He presented an ass cheek. "You know I love it when you spank me."

She growled, heading for the bedroom. "You have a one-track mind sometimes."

He struck a pose just for himself. "Is that wrong?"

"Not unless we've got plans."

He double-checked himself then inhaled quickly at the sight of the love of his life as she stepped into the bathroom, a stylish yet casual outfit accentuating her fit frame. "My God you're gorgeous."

She beamed a smile at him then gave him a peck on the cheek. "Thanks!" She checked her watch. "Let's go, we're going to be late."

Kane patted her bum as they left the confines of the bathroom. "It's not like there's going to be any traffic." They stepped out of their apartment and into the hallway. "Want to squeeze in a quickie on the elevator?"

She flipped him the bird.

"Huh, I didn't think that was a thing in China."

"I'm picking up new habits." She motioned toward the stairwell. "Let's take the stairs. I skipped my workout. Every bit counts."

"I wasn't workout enough for you?"

She winked at him. "Baby, you've seen me work out. What do you think?"

He had to acknowledge her point, no matter how much it might bruise his ego. Her workouts were intense. Incredibly intense. Far beyond anything he ever did. It accounted for her stunning body, every muscle and sinew on display when she was at full tilt, yet not bulging so as to make him think he might have a short dude in the sack with him. "I invoke my Fifth Amendment right to remain silent."

She grinned then opened the door. He reached out and grabbed her arm, a voice echoing through the stairwell, a voice out of place.

It was too business like.

He pulled her back into the hallway then cautiously stepped forward, his ear cocked, listening for anything, though hearing nothing but his own breathing. He silently stepped to the rail and looked down, then jerked back at the sight of a man in a business suit standing two floors down.

At Leroux's landing.

And it was someone he recognized.

"What is it?" whispered Fang.

"I think I might have figured out who sent that message."

Leroux/White Residence, Fairfax Towers

Falls Church, Virginia

CIA Analyst Supervisor Chris Leroux sat on his couch, fidgeting, while his far-too-hot-for-him girlfriend, CIA Agent Sherrie White, sat comfortably beside him, smiling at their unexpected guest.

His boss.

Their boss.

National Clandestine Service Chief for the CIA, Leif Morrison, a man who had never set foot here before tonight.

And had said little since arriving only minutes ago.

Leroux stared at his watch again. "I'm sure they'll be here any moment, sir."

"I'm sure they will. I should have timed my arrival to take into account your friend's propensity for being late when having access to a beautiful woman."

Sherrie laughed. "You definitely know your agents, sir."

Morrison nodded. "Just the good ones."

Leroux noticed Sherrie tense slightly. He put an arm over her shoulders and she leaned into him. "Kane is definitely the best."

Morrison continued to stare at them, as if sizing them up for some test. "I've been following your career, Agent, with interest."

Sherrie stiffened. "Yes, sir, thank you, sir."

"You're up for promotion."

Leroux's eyes widened. "Really?"

She glanced up at him. "You're surprised?"

He shook his head. "No, but you hadn't mentioned it."

"I didn't want to jinx it."

There was a knock on the door, coded.

"That's Dylan." Leroux leaped to his feet and answered the door. Kane and Fang stood there, Fang with a bottle of wine in her hand, Kane with a look that told Leroux his friend already knew they had an unexpected visitor, and that he knew exactly whom it was. "Umm, glad you could make it?"

Fang gave him a hug and peck on the cheek, then headed deeper into the apartment as he and Kane exchanged a quick thumping hug.

"Good to see you, buddy. Do you entertain the Chief often?"

Leroux chuckled, closing the door and locking it. "We have a standing dinner date once a week. Didn't you know?"

Kane grinned, slapping him on the back before stepping into the living area where Fang and Morrison were shaking hands, Morrison playing a critical role in the asylum agreement between Fang and the United States government.

"I'm pleased to see you've made a life for yourself here."

Fang bowed slightly. "Thanks to you."

Morrison returned to his chair, waving an arm at Leroux and Kane. "I think there are others more responsible than myself."

Kane took her hand and they occupied their usual position on the loveseat as Leroux returned to his perch beside Sherrie.

Morrison leaned forward. "I won't waste any more of your time than I have to, though I'm afraid your evening's plans might need to be rescheduled should you heed my request."

Leroux's eyes widened slightly. "Anything, sir."

Morrison smiled. "You might not be so quick to accept, once I tell you what I'm about to tell you."

Kane exchanged a glance with his friend. "And why's that?"

"Because what I'm about to tell you, I have never told a soul in over thirty years."

Everyone leaned forward in anticipation, Leroux drawing in a shaky breath. "You can trust us, sir."

"I wouldn't be here if I didn't trust each of you implicitly."

Fang rose. "Perhaps I should leave. You barely know—"

Morrison raised a hand, cutting her off. "Miss Lee, if my agents trust you with their lives, agents I have the utmost faith in, then I too will trust you." He raised a finger, cutting off anything else from being said as he stared at each of them. "But I will tell you this. If you remain in this room, you will be privy to information that could mean the death of all of us, unless we can stop what has already begun."

Leroux's heart hammered and Sherrie's fingernails dug into his leg.

"If any of you want to leave now, please do so, with my blessing. No one will think any less of you, I assure you."

Kane flicked his wrist at the statement. "You know me, sir, I've never run away from a fight."

"Me neither," said Sherrie.

Fang sat back down. "I would relish any opportunity to help, sir."

All eyes turned to Leroux. "Umm, well, it is my apartment, so I can't really leave, can I?"

Morrison leaned forward, everyone's attention firmly on him. His heart rate was up a few notches, and he wasn't certain if there was any one thing to point to for the cause. Was he scared? A little. He was prepared to die for his country when he was a young man, but those days of being an agent out in the field were long behind him. Decades behind him.

And now he had a family.

Whoever was behind the poisoning in Salisbury hadn't cared about collateral damage. If they were going to kill him, then fine, but he couldn't risk his wife or children getting hurt, or worse, in the process.

And he didn't know who he could trust beyond those in this room.

He started with a little levity to break the tension that gripped his audience. "This is before your time, but there used to be a country called the Soviet Union."

Kane's eyebrows shot up. "Really? Tell us more!" His voice was one of mock eagerness, and loud exhales and smiles suggested Morrison's tactic had worked.

"In 1988, there was the Moscow Summit. It was a rare meeting in Moscow between Soviet and American leaders, and marked a turning point in the Cold War that had been underway since shortly after the end of the Second World War. Within three years of this summit, the Soviet Union had collapsed, and the Cold War was over."

"Only to be replaced with a new one," muttered Leroux.

Morrison agreed. The current state of Russian-American affairs was bleak, with no end to the hostilities in sight, but that wasn't his concern at the moment. "As a result, the Union of Soviet Socialist Republics dissolved, their military was left to crumble, and their economy, already a basket case, teetered on the brink of collapse. In time, they turned things around, and are once again a threat to world peace. But in 1988, the Soviet Union was still very much a threat, very much a superpower, and very much divided over their future." He regarded each of them as he paused. "So divided, that there was a plot to assassinate the Soviet leader, Mikhail Gorbachev."

Kane leaned back in his chair. "Why is this the first we're hearing of it?"

"Because officially, it never happened."

Leroux's eyes narrowed. "Then how do you know about it?"

Morrison sighed. "Because I was there."

Kane cursed. "What do you mean you were there? There as in you witnessed it, or there as in—"

"I helped stop it."

Sherrie smiled. "Director Morrison, super spy!"

Morrison shook his head. "Nope, super lucky. If it weren't for another agent, I'd have died that day, on my first out of country assignment. Listen carefully, because this is all I know, despite my security clearance. I was on patrol with my assigned Soviet counterpart. He spotted someone, a former member of the KGB, who shouldn't be within the secure zone. I tried to radio it in, but our frequency was jammed and hijacked, fake status reports being transmitted including one in my own voice. My Soviet counterpart went to seek guidance at the command post while I pursued the man. I discovered two dead agents inside a building that had been evacuated for a staged public appearance by the two leaders in Red Square. I went upstairs, engaged the assassin, and was stopped by a gun to my back by a third person."

Kane whistled. "How the hell did you get out of that?"

"The man I was pursuing assumed this person was on his side, and proceeded to set up his sniper rifle to take the shot, when the third man asked what color suit the target was wearing."

"Powder blue," whispered Leroux.

Morrison's eyebrows shot up. "How did you know that?"

"I watched a video on YouTube about it recently. I can't remember why, just one of those rabbit holes you sometimes go down."

"Well, you're right. The answer was powder blue. And that's where it got interesting."

Fang cleared her throat. "Umm, it's not interesting yet?"

Morrison smiled. "The agent who got the drop on me then said something like, 'So Gorbachev is the target.' He said it as if he hadn't known. This was when the man I was pursuing realized something was wrong, and the third guy put two bullets into his back."

"So, he was American?" asked Leroux.

"At the time, I wasn't sure. He just told me to get the hell out of there, tell no one of what I had seen, and that neither of us was ever there."

"So, what did you do?"

"I got my ass back outside, never found my Russian partner, and just kept my mouth shut. Nobody asked me anything, the summit ended, and I tried to forget what had, or hadn't, happened."

Kane scratched his neck. "Umm, one question."

Morrison chuckled. "Just one?"

Kane grunted. "Okay, one to start. Were we sharing frequencies with the Soviets?"

Morrison smiled at the astute question. "No, we weren't."

"So then, our frequency was not only jammed, not only hijacked with fake status reports, but also those facts were never mentioned?"

"Exactly." Morrison held up a finger. "Though, keep in mind, I was a junior agent, not even a rung on the ladder of the chain of command. I have to think there were some questions being asked after the fact, but with nothing having 'happened'"—he delivered air quotes—"then I have to assume it was dropped."

Leroux took a sip of his Diet Dr. Pepper. "With your clearance level now, surely you could read the file."

Morrison nodded. "I could. And I did. And there's nothing in it."

"Huh?"

"Exactly. No mention of anything with our comms being interfered with beyond a single reference to the Soviets following most of the agreed upon protocols with several minor exceptions noted in an addendum that was on a corrupted floppy disk."

Leroux returned his glass to the table. "That suggests someone with a significant clearance level was behind this. At least the American side of it."

Morrison regarded him. "That's an interesting way of putting it. Why do you think there are two sides?"

Leroux flushed slightly, the poor young man still not brimming with the confidence someone of his skills should be, though significantly improved over the past couple of years, thanks in no small part to the beautiful agent sitting at his side whose heart he had somehow captured. "Well, isn't it obvious? Your partner spotted an ex-KGB agent inside the secure zone, who then tried to kill Gorbachev. That means Soviet elements were involved at some level."

"Agreed."

"And our comms would have been secure, so any jamming or hijacking had to come from either our end or the Soviet end, but the fact there's no mention in the report suggests a cover-up at a senior level, at least senior level on the ground. And that means someone on our side was involved."

"Again, agreed, though it could be as simple as someone covering up the discrepancies after the fact, since the Soviet Union collapsed regardless." Morrison motioned to the four glasses on the table. "Can I get a drink?"

Kane raised a finger. "Scotch?" he suggested with a hopeful smile.

Morrison chuckled. "I think we're going to all need clear heads for the foreseeable future. Just water is fine with me."

Leroux rose to get it when Sherrie patted his leg. "I'll get it. Something tells me you're going to be more involved than I am." She left for the kitchen, Morrison smiling his thanks.

"Now, here's one little piece of critical information I wasn't able to garner until I became Director."

Sherrie returned, handing him a glass of ice cold water. "I hope you like ice."

Morrison nodded, taking a sip, his throat parched. "Love it, thanks." He put the glass down on a coaster that Leroux slid across the table. "I found out who saved my ass."

Kane's head bobbed with a smile. "You found the third man."

"Yes. And you know him."

Kane's eyebrows rose. "Excuse me?"

"I never got his name, but I could never forget that face. The first chance I got, I went through all the agent files from that time. He wasn't on the official detail sent with Reagan, but he was an active agent assigned to the region."

Kane threw up his hands. "You're killing me, boss. Who was it?"

"Alex West."

Both Kane and Leroux fell back in their seats, their jaws dropping, while their other halves exchanged glances with each other. Sherrie asked first. "Who's Alex West?"

Kane and Leroux stared at the carpet.

Fang's mouth opened slightly, her eyes widening in recognition, and Morrison was about to question his top agent's ability to keep his mouth shut. "Wasn't he Batman?"

Kane snorted and Morrison suppressed a smile as her boyfriend corrected her. "Umm, that was *Adam* West, hon. And how did you know that?"

"He died recently."

Kane's eyes shot wide. "He's dead! When the hell did that happen?"

"When you were on assignment, I guess." She held up a hand. "I think we're getting off topic. Who is *Alex* West?"

Morrison turned to her . "If we're going to figure out what's going on, we'll have to have no secrets between the five of us. Alex West was one of our top agents for years, and was nearing the end of his career in 1988."

She nodded at the silent parties. "And how do these two know an agent that old?"

"The Gray Network."

Fang's eyes shot wide as her chin dropped. "Huh? Is that a fifty-shades for seniors thing?"

It was Morrison's turn to snort, memories coming back of his wife reading the books in bed, the line thankfully drawn at not seeing the movies. "No, it's not a septuagenarian sex club, it's an unofficial network of retired personnel, mostly CIA and other Western agents and staffers, that keep an eye on things using contacts built up over decades that trust them, but not 'us.'"

Fang shook her head. "I had no idea."

"Most don't."

She looked at Leroux. "How do you know about them?"

"They approached me a few years ago with respect to those Russian nuclear suitcase bombs."

Kane took a drink. "And I met some of them in Germany, and we conducted an op in France."

Fang's eyes widened. "They're still doing ops?"

Kane nodded emphatically. "It was actually quite impressive, frankly."

Morrison raised a hand, cutting everyone off. "Again, we're getting off topic. Special Agent West was the man who stopped the assassination attempt that day, ordered me to keep my mouth shut, and obviously helped cover up whatever happened."

"Have you talked to him about it?" asked Sherrie.

Morrison shook his head. "Just ask Dylan how difficult it was to see him in the first place."

Kane leaned back, putting his arm across the back of the loveseat. "He's a hermit in the Black Forest, excellent security, with a propensity to shoot first and ask questions later. Nice guy. Still got a little lead in the pencil, I think."

Fang stared at him. "Lead in the pencil?"

Morrison regained control. "Anyway, I haven't spoken to him since that day, but the mere fact he was there, and seemed to know what was going on, suggests he knows far more than I do."

Sherrie nodded. "Sounds like a good place to start."

Kane lifted a finger. "Umm, second question. Start what? Why are we having this conversation over thirty years after the fact? What's changed?"

Morrison frowned. "My Soviet partner, and his daughter, were poisoned in Salisbury today, and he had a note in his wallet with my home phone number on it and my old callsign for the mission."

Kane cursed. "Poisoned? How?"

"Details are sketchy. They're thinking it was a nerve agent. Possibly Novichok related."

Leroux's eyebrows shot up. "Holy crap! That's serious stuff. *State* level stuff. You can't just cook this stuff up in your basement."

Kane grunted in agreement. "Not to mention the fact it's a Russian concoction."

"Exactly," said Morrison. "If that was indeed the nerve agent used, you can bet this was state sanctioned."

A blast of air escaped Sherrie's lips. "That takes some serious brass balls to assassinate a former Russian agent on foreign soil. *British* soil."

"Agreed."

Leroux shook his head. "This makes no sense. Why would you use a nerve agent directly traceable back to the source? If this is confirmed, there will be *zero* doubt that the Russians are behind it. It's idiocy!"

Morrison regarded his prize analyst. His gut instinct on things was legendary, and it was why he had been given a team of his own to facilitate the beautiful mind trapped behind too many insecurities. "That's exactly what I was thinking. What does your famous gut tell you?"

Leroux paused, an idle finger tapping rapidly on his knee as everyone remained silent, staring at him. "I think we're dealing with one of two things. Well, three things, but I think we can exclude sheer idiocy."

Kane grunted. "I wouldn't be so sure about that."

Leroux continued. "First, it is the Russians, as in the Kremlin, and they're sending a message. If the guy just turned up dead with a bullet to the head, then it would be chalked up as murder and it wouldn't even make the news. Poison him like this, it makes international news, and everyone they want to send a message to receives it."

"You certainly did, sir."

Morrison nodded at Kane. "I certainly did." He turned back to Leroux. "And second?"

"That someone is trying to make it *look* like the Russian government is involved, and they aren't at all."

Morrison sighed, his underling coming to the same conclusions he had. "So, where do we start? If we ask the Russian government, they'll just deny it either way. There's no way they'll admit that a nerve agent that lethal was stolen, and they'll never admit they used it."

Kane shook his head. "Either way, a message was being sent. We need to find out who to, and the only way we're going to be able to do that is to find out who *might* want to send a message. We're assuming that this has something to do with 1988. We don't know that. The only reason we're thinking that is because you happened to know the victim, and he happened to have your number in his wallet." His eyes narrowed. "Why was that, do you think?"

Morrison frowned. "There's one tidbit I forgot to mention."

"Which is?"

"The exact text of that note." He pulled out his notes from the phone call. "It said, and I quote, 'If something odd should happen, call this number, and tell him Whiskey-Alpha-Four-One needs help from Whiskey-Alpha-Four-Two.'"

Kane leaned back. "And you're Whiskey-Alpha-Four-Two?"

"Yes."

Sherrie shook her head. "But how could he know in advance to reach out to you?"

"And how did he have your home number?" added Fang.

Leroux's face had the distant stare that so often meant he was figuring something out. He smiled slightly to himself, then returned his attention to Morrison. "Because there was only ever one thing in his life that he thought he might be killed for."

Morrison's head bobbed, as did everyone else's. It was so simple, it had to be true. He had looked up Kulick when he was granted clearance, and couldn't find him. He wasn't in the files about the operation, so his name had either been scrubbed, or the false identity provided for him had been untraceable. A junior agent like that would never have such a clean identity wasted on him, which likely meant there was nothing to find after the fact.

His career had either ended that day, or he had been quickly sidelined, and in the chaos of the collapse of the Soviet Union, he had been lost, eventually ending up in England with his family.

Leroux had to be right.

Morrison summarized. "So, we have a junior agent who did nothing remarkable in his career, and knows it. The only thing he was ever exposed to was the assassination plot, so he knows that if anything ever happens to him, it has to be related to that. The only person he knows from that incident that he can trust is me, since I tried to stop it. I become a public figure with my position, he recognizes me at some point in time, then uses his connections to get my home number. He puts it in his wallet for someone to find, just in case." He cursed. "If only we could talk to him."

Kane's eyes narrowed. "He's not dead?"

Morrison shook his head. "No. They're both in comas, apparently."

"Then with him out of the picture, and you with nothing beyond what you saw as a junior agent, I see no other choice. We have to talk to West, and find out what he knows."

Morrison nodded. "Agreed. But I can't exactly send an agent to Germany without a paper trail."

Kane grinned. "Oh, I have my ways, sir."

Morrison chuckled. "You wouldn't be much of an agent if you didn't. Do I want to know?"

"Nope."

"Very well. Get your ass to Germany and meet with West. Find out what he knows."

Sherrie leaned forward, eagerness on her face. "What about the UK? You'll need someone there you can trust in case they regain consciousness. Maybe to look into things quietly?"

Morrison agreed, but Sherrie was about to be disappointed with his idea. "We need someone we can trust in the UK, someone on the outside."

Kane appeared to catch on immediately. "Someone with connections, who could poke around without raising any questions, but that we could trust implicitly?"

"Exactly."

Leroux's jaw dropped. "You're not thinking about who I think you're thinking about."

Morrison nodded. "I think we're all thinking the same thing."

Sherrie glanced at Fang. "Umm, I don't think we're *all* thinking the same thing."

Fang agreed. "I haven't the foggiest."

Kane didn't help. "But that's a big ask. Do you think he'd say yes?"

Morrison shrugged. "I think he would if it came from the right person. Also, we can't risk any contact with him tracing back to us."

Kane pursed his lips, a burst of air escaping. "Well, I know him to a point, but that's always been when dealing with his best friend. To ask him to help, well, frankly, sir, *you,* is a really big ask. It could be dangerous, and it could affect his career."

Morrison had to agree with everything Kane was saying, though his agent was missing one critical element. "You're forgetting one thing."

"What?"

"That's he's a cop, and he's always been a cop. Just the fact this happened in his country will make him want to get involved."

Kane sighed, leaning back on the couch. "I don't know, though I think you're right about our best chances. I can ask, I guess. What's the worst that could happen?"

Sherrie threw her hands up. "Who the hell are you two talking about? Agent Reading?"

Kane tapped his nose.

"And this other person?"

"An old friend. I'll drop by on the way to Germany and ask him to reach out."

"Do that." Morrison turned to Leroux. "We have another problem."

"What's that?"

"We're going to need intel, and we can't use CIA resources for that, or your team."

Leroux stared at his laptop sitting nearby. "Umm, I don't think Google is going to cut it."

Kane held up a hand. "I think I can help there."

Morrison shook his head. "I don't want to know."

Leroux looked at Kane. "We'll talk offline." He turned back to Morrison. "But I think I'm going to need help."

Morrison chewed his cheek for a moment. "Who'd you have in mind?"

"Sonya. I trust her implicitly. I'll read her in only on what she needs to know, leaving your name out of it for as long as I can."

"What about Randy?" asked Sherrie. "He seems to be a sharp cookie."

Leroux shook his head. "With no brain-mouth filter. He's liable to let the whole thing slip one day while he's spinning in his chair." He shook his head again. "No, this needs someone calmer, more experienced, and that's Sonya."

Kane winked. "You two, working alone in cramped quarters. Do you think she can handle it?"

Morrison suppressed a chuckle, well aware that the attractive yet awkward Sonya Tong had a crush on her supervisor. He wondered if Sherrie knew.

She frowned, apparently in the loop. "Maybe I should chaperone."

Boykov Residence

Moscow, Russia

Vasily Boykov cursed at the bottom of yet another bottle of vodka. There was a time when he celebrated the occurrence, but now it was just another disappointment in his miserable life. When he was young, vodka was the reward for the end of a hard day's work, the elixir that took the edge off a cold morning, or the tonic that cured all that ailed the hardworking man.

But now, it was just another indicator of how miserable his day-to-day existence was, for all the wonders that was the drink of vodka years ago, what was truly special about it was the fact it was almost always done with friends.

Something he had few of anymore.

In fact, he could think of none.

For he was on the losing side.

He had been committed to the cause, committed to the preservation of the Soviet way of life, and had failed. Not only had he failed in his task to assassinate the traitor Gorbachev, but he had been shot twice in the back and left for dead by some American scumbag who was supposed to be on his side. Why the man had betrayed him in the final moments was something he had been asking for over thirty years, yet the motivation was as irrelevant now as it was then.

He had betrayed him, and that was all that mattered.

If I ever see the bastard again, I'll kill him.

Yet the likelihood of that was zero or worse.

He had been found by his own men and his life saved, and ironically it was the collapse of the Soviet Union that ultimately saved his life. If the USSR had survived, he would have been executed by his own people, or sent to a gulag to toil the remainder of his days.

But instead, he was simply forgotten. Forgotten by the few involved in the conspiracy. And forgotten by the government that replaced the one he had served loyally for so many years.

He had a small pension given to all men his age, nothing to show for his years of service and loyalty, a dearth of friends, and no family. He had nothing but an apartment in a building that should have been condemned a decade ago, and yet another empty bottle of vodka.

And even it had little effect on him now, beyond giving him the shakes should he not acquire a new one.

His life wasn't worth living.

He stared at the old television, Soviet-era engineering, and frowned at the barely visible hockey game. The speaker still worked, at least as well as it ever had, and it was his only company, though a radio would be as effective. It was the warm glow it gave at night, the talking box the best friend he had, and when it finally died, he had no money to replace it.

When it dies, I die.

It would be easy enough. He had his old Makarov pistol in his nightstand drawer. He kept it clean. And loaded. At first, it was for security. He feared someone someday might come knocking, cleaning up a decades-old mess, then it was for the thieves after the near collapse of law and order when the Soviet Empire dissolved. But even thieves need a payoff, and he had nothing to steal, so they had left him alone for years.

Now it was his escape hatch should he decide enough was enough.

His phone rang, startling him. He couldn't recall the last time it had actually made a sound, and had forgotten he had it. He pushed from his threadbare chair and winced at the pain left behind by two bullets in the back and seventy years of hard living. He lifted the receiver from the wall by the small kitchenette.

"Da?"

"Is this Vasily Boykov?"

His eyes narrowed at the woman's voice, a voice mentioning a name he hadn't heard spoken in a very long time. The hair on the back of his neck stood. "You should know, you called me. What do you want?"

"I just wanted to make sure you were home."

There was a click and the line went dead.

And he cursed, dropping the handset as he rushed toward his nightstand and the Makarov he had never thought he'd use for its true purpose again. He had known he would likely soon die, though he had assumed by a bullet to the head, a bullet he'd deliver himself.

This was a welcome if unexpected change to his future plans.

But to give him a warning?

That was just sporting.

And made little sense in today's Russia.

He would be dead in the next few minutes, a team of four likely on its way up the stairs as he double-checked his weapon. If he were lucky, he'd get one, maybe two, though not all of them.

But at least he'd go out fighting.

It was just unfortunate that his exit wasn't under his control, as he had wanted. He had been looking forward to putting his own bullet in his head, and had come close on several drunken occasions, but something had always kept him going. Some memory, something on the television, some upcoming hockey game he wanted to see. The reasons were sometimes trivial, sometimes noble, sometimes nostalgic.

Yet despite the fact he wanted to die, his training from all those years ago demanded he make a fight of it.

For Yury Minkin couldn't win.

The bastard deserves to die.

They had all been called into a room with no windows, a room with dim lights, a room guaranteed to have no listening devices, a room they were to never speak of having been in after the briefing was concluded.

A room with no names spoken.

Yet faces had been seen.

Including the traitor who had shot him in the back.

He would recognize them all today if they were paraded in front of him, yet he had never seen any of them again.

Except Minkin.

On the television, that wretched lone friend that had once again given him a reason to live after a news report aired about another oligarch arrested for fraud by the testosterone-fueled leader of their great nation. He had heard the name many times, the uber-rich a fascination among the public and its news outlets, but in a room with no names, it had meant nothing to him.

Until that night several weeks ago, when he finally had a face to put with the name, a face he'd recognize even thirty years later.

He had put down the gun.

And the vodka.

He needed to remember clearly.

But there was little to remember, beyond the fact that Minkin was the man giving the briefing to the half-dozen in the room.

Half a dozen men determined to preserve a way of life.

Half a dozen Soviets *and* Americans, who wanted nothing to do with Gorbachev's glasnost and perestroika.

There was a loud bang below him followed by a rumbling.

What the hell is this?

The single room that had been his life for too long shook, the already crumbling plaster cracking, dust filling the air in the dim light cast by his lone lamp and the television, when suddenly he was thrust into darkness, the power failing.

They weren't going to shoot him after all.

He leaped for the bed, the adrenaline-fueled move surprising even himself, and grabbed one edge of the thin mattress, rolling it over him as the entire floor fell out from under him. He cursed then reached out for the nightstand, falling with his bed, and grasped inside the partially open drawer, gripping the cold steel of his trusted Makarov.

Then he abruptly came to a halt, the bed frame creaking in protest as the weight of his body pressed against it then sprung back up.

But it wasn't over.

The roof hadn't arrived yet.

He braced as the din of collapsing concrete and twisting steel overwhelmed his senses, the air thick with pulverized stone making his breathing more labored than it normally was.

Then there was silence, nothing moving for several seconds before a creaking sound directly above his mattress betrayed what was about to come. He released his grip on the mattress and it flopped aside, the debris it had protected him from nothing compared to what was only inches from his face.

A steel beam supporting what appeared to be a significant portion of the roof, starlight visible in some sections that had completely collapsed.

Along with the still standing walls of the two apartment blocks that had bookended his own.

The creak sounded again and the mass above him moved slightly.

Shit!

He rolled out of the bed, now at a precarious angle, and cursed as he lost his footing, sliding down what was once the floor of his apartment and into a mass of debris before coming to an abrupt, painful halt.

Then he heard the moans and cries of the denizens he had ignored for years, the victims of a plot to kill him.

But why? Why was it necessary to kill so many just to get him? There were ways to kill people that were far less messy.

This was amateurish.

Or it was meant to send a message.

But to whom? If he was indeed being targeted by those involved in the plot all those years ago, it made no sense. None of them knew each other, therefore who was out there to receive the message?

Though perhaps that wasn't true.

He didn't know who anyone was, except for Minkin, and that was only a recent discovery. But the others? He had no idea who they were.

Perhaps they were in the know more than he was back then, or their stations had changed and were now privy to information a disgraced, disavowed spy didn't have access to. He was the tool being used by whoever was pulling the strings back then. He had been "kicked out" of the KGB, the cover story spread among the ranks so if he were caught it could never be traced back to the organization he had been fiercely loyal to. He was given the task of actually pulling the trigger, of killing the agents guarding the building, including the one who had been in the room during the briefing, responsible for getting him inside.

He was the one who would be blamed should things go wrong.

But if everything had gone right, the Americans would have been blamed. It was an American rifle, American ammunition. It was the Americans whose frequencies had been hijacked, something that could only be done by their own people.

In the chaos that would have ensued, each side would be blaming the other, and the Cold War would have continued unabated for decades more, and Mother Russia wouldn't now be the shadow of what it once was.

"Help me!"

It was a small voice that ended his reverie. A tiny voice.

A child's voice.

Sirens in the distance were getting closer now, and as he sat up, moving his arms and legs, wincing from the cuts and bruises but thankful for the lack of broken bones, anger set in at what had been done.

Whoever was behind this, and he was almost certain it was Minkin, had to be punished.

Though how he, a broken septuagenarian, could mete out any level of punishment, was beyond him.

He gripped his Makarov, still firmly in his hand, and pushed to his feet, gingerly making his way down the thirty feet of piled debris, and to the road below.

With one final mission that had nothing to do with the State, the Party, or Communism.

Only revenge.

And he could think of only one place to begin.

Acton/Palmer Residence

St. Paul, Maryland

"Mai just texted, they'll be here in fifteen minutes."

Archaeology Professor James Acton muttered a curse as he worked the ground beef with his fingers, mixing in the freshly cut onions and green peppers, along with the breadcrumbs and his secret blend of spices for the homemade hamburgers they would be grilling shortly. It was chilly outside, though an unexpected jump in the temperature had changed their plans from Laura's pasta to his burgers, even if it meant shoveling a path to the barbecue.

A warm spell in Maryland should never go to waste.

And he had a hankering for barbecued burgers.

His wife and love of his life swept into the room, still taking his breath away. Laura Palmer was an accomplished archaeologist herself, and they had met under fire in London several years ago, a relationship kindled that never waned. "Almost done with those burgers?"

"Almost. You're in charge of the salads, right?"

"Yup." She sat on one of the stools at their breakfast bar and poured a glass of wine. She held up the bottle. "Want one?"

"Ahh, yes, and are those salads going to prepare themselves, my dear?"

She poured him a glass then gave him a look as she pushed it toward his meaty fingers. "I, unlike you, didn't take a nap this afternoon, so I, unlike you, got my work done early, so I, unlike you, could relax before they arrived and watch you panic."

He flipped her a beef covered bird.

And the doorbell rang.

"I thought you said fifteen minutes?"

Laura's eyes narrowed. "I did." She rose and headed for the door, the alarm chiming a moment later. He heard a mumbled conversation, Spotify playing through an Echo device in the kitchen drowning out anything recognizable as he prepared the food.

The playlist hit Panama, and all hope was lost.

He squeezed, punched, and smacked the beef mixture while banging his head, wishing he had long hair if only for these next few minutes, and nearly jumped three feet when a throat cleared.

"Should we leave you alone while you beat your meat?"

A smile spread at the sight of his former student, Dylan Kane.

"Alexa, stop."

Kane looked disappointed. "I would have waited. Great tune."

Acton grinned. "Serves his country, and has great taste in music." He paused, staring at him. "While I love seeing you, Dylan, you never come without problems."

Kane chuckled and took a seat at the breakfast bar, waving off the offer of wine from Laura. "Unfortunately, this is a quick pop-in to ask a favor of you. Or more accurately, a favor of a friend of yours."

Acton's eyes narrowed. Kane was CIA, a special agent. He was in the thick of the most dangerous things imaginable, and if he needed a favor, it had to be a big one. "Go on."

"First, I'll apologize upfront for being vague. The less you know, the better. Suffice it to say, we have a situation that's rapidly developing, and those of us involved aren't sure who we can trust. We need someone on the outside in the UK to do some work for us."

"You mean Hugh."

Kane nodded at Laura. "Exactly."

Acton frowned. "Why not contact him directly?"

"Well, it's a big ask, so we felt it coming from you might be better, but also, we can't have anything tracing back to us. A call from you to him, if ever traced, isn't unusual and would be ignored. From one of us, or worse, one of our secure lines, could raise flags down the road."

Acton worked the excess beef off his fingers. "This sounds dangerous."

"It could be, I'm afraid." Kane sighed. "I'll give you a hint. You've heard about what happened in Salisbury yesterday?"

Laura immediately replied, the UK her old stomping grounds. "You mean those poisonings, and all those emergency personnel getting sick as well?"

Kane smiled. "Two for two. It involves that."

Acton tensed. "This involves the Russians, doesn't it?"

Kane regarded him for a moment. "I can't confirm that, but you're a smart man, Doc."

"So why does the CIA need the help of an Interpol agent? Don't you have people there?"

"Like I said, we don't know who we can trust. I really can't say anything beyond that for your own safety."

Acton shook his head. "Look, I'll be happy to make the call and let Hugh decide, but he's going to want to know more than what you've told me if he's going to put his life on the line."

"And I'll fill him in with whatever is operationally necessary." Kane leaned forward. "Look, at the moment, there are only five people who know what's going on, not including you two, because I'm intentionally leaving you in the dark. I'm going to be running an off-the-books op, outside the CIA, to try and save lives, and hopefully prevent any more attacks like what happened in Salisbury yesterday."

"So, it was an attack?" asked Laura.

"Absolutely."

"And it was the Russians?"

Kane chuckled. "And you're a smart woman, so I'll leave it to the both of you to speculate. I'm leaving the country shortly, and I don't know when I'll be back. We're doing this with a minimal team, so things are going to be difficult, especially with only two techs supporting me, but we just can't use Agency personnel or equipment."

Acton's eyes narrowed and his heart rate picked up as an idea occurred to him. Then he shelved it.

"What?"

Acton flinched. "Huh?"

"I recognize that look, Doc, you had an idea."

Acton shook his head. "It was nothing. Well, it was nothing I'd care to say out loud."

"Spill it."

Acton looked at Laura for a moment then sighed. "I was thinking about someone who might be able to help."

Laura shook her head, jabbing a finger into the counter. "Absolutely not!"

"I know, which is why I stopped myself."

Kane frowned, then glanced at his watch. "Listen, Doc, if you knew what was going on, you'd realize that there's no time to waste, and that lives are at stake. If you know of someone who can help, tell me, so we can at least discuss it."

Acton sighed, and Laura threw up her hands. "Fine. Tell him."

"Tommy Granger. He's a grad student of mine who is a whiz with computers, and can hack pretty much anything you can dream of."

Kane's eyebrows rose slightly. "Yeah, I remember him. He's the kid who hacked the DoD mainframe when he was like twelve or something."

"Something like that."

Kane's head bobbed slowly as he leaned back in his stool, folding his arms across his chest. "He could be perfect. It would mean we could always have two people providing support, instead of one every shift."

Laura shook her head. "And I said no. There's no way I'm letting Tommy get involved."

"Letting me get involved in what?"

Acton and Laura both flinched, though Kane didn't even look behind him, as if he already knew their houseguests had arrived.

Laura hopped from her stool and rushed forward, giving both Tommy and his girlfriend, Mai Trinh, hugs. "I'm so sorry, we didn't hear you come in."

Mai flushed. "We were going to ring the doorbell, but Tommy insisted you kept saying to just come in, so…"

Laura gave the diminutive Vietnamese girl another hug and a kiss on the top of her head. "You two are always welcome to just walk in."

Acton cleared his throat. "Well, only if we're expecting you. We might be in the middle of some sweet lovin' or something you wouldn't want to walk in on."

Kane snorted and Tommy moved in for a fist bump but was waved off. "Sorry, I'm still covered in meat." Acton headed for the sink and washed his hands, then properly greeted their guests. He gestured at Kane. "This is an old student of mine, Dylan Kane."

Handshakes were exchanged.

Tommy looked at them. "So, what were you talking about? I heard my name!"

Acton and Laura exchanged glances. Laura started. "Well, Tommy, umm…" She paused, throwing up her hands. "Dylan, I don't know what I can say!"

Kane laughed then turned to Tommy. "I'm an operator with the Special Activities Division of the Special Operations Group in the Central Intelligence Agency."

Mai gasped and Tommy's jaw dropped. "That is so freakin' cool!"

Kane grinned. "It is."

Mai appeared confused. "What does that mean? You're a spy?"

Apparently not so confused.

"Yes. I kill people for a living, and by doing so, save many more lives in the process."

Tommy paled slightly. "And you want me to get involved somehow?"

"I need a computer whiz for an off-the-books op. Anything you see or do will be strictly secret, and you can never talk about it with anyone, including your friends, lovers, priests, rabbis, whatever."

Tommy gulped. "Umm, okay?"

Mai wrapped around Tommy's arm. "Is it dangerous?"

Kane regarded her for a moment. "I'm not going to lie to you. Anything in my business is dangerous. However, you'll be working in a secret location barely an hour from here, only half a dozen trusted people will know where you are, and even fewer will know *who* you are. When it's over, you walk away, and I'll make sure it's worth your while."

"You mean I'll get paid?"

"Handsomely."

Acton leaned forward. "I thought you said this is off-the-books? How are you paying him?"

Kane eyed him. "What are you, his agent?"

Acton chuckled. "No, I'm not doubting you, I'm just curious."

"Let's just say I've got funds tucked away for rainy days like this."

Laura frowned. "And just how rainy is it?"

Kane looked at her. "It could be very rainy for a good friend of mine."

"I'll do it!"

Everyone turned to Tommy. Mai was the first to break the silence.

"Are you insane?"

Tommy shook his head, but his entire body was trembling, and his wide eyes suggested he too was shocked at what had come out of his mouth.

"You don't have to," said Kane, apparently recognizing the fear. "We'll manage without you."

Tommy shook his head then inhaled deeply, steadying himself. "No, I want to help. Ever since I was arrested, I've wanted to try and make up for what I did. I want to do this. I *need* to do this."

Kane slapped him on the shoulder, the poor kid almost shrieking in terror. "Kid, if you do this, I think you'll have more than made up for any past transgressions."

Tommy's eyes shot wide, his fear forgotten. "Do you think I'd be able to get a job at the CIA?"

Kane turned to Acton and Laura, jerking a thumb at Tommy. "Look at this guy, already renegotiating." He rose then grabbed a notepad and pen sitting by the phone, quickly jotting down something. He pressed it into Tommy's hand. "Don't show this to anyone. Don't program it into any GPS. Don't Google the address. Just know how to get there. When you get there, give it to the man in charge."

Tommy shook out a nod, trembling once again. "Y-yes, sir."

Kane turned to Acton. "You'll make that call?"

"Right away." He paused. "And if he says yes?"

"Have him contact me through the secure app."

Acton nodded then gestured toward Tommy. "Can he at least stay for burgers before he leaves?"

"Of course." Kane checked his watch. "How fast can you rustle me up a couple to go?"

"Alexa, fire up the grill."

Hugh Reading Residence

Whitehall, London, England

Interpol Agent Hugh Reading had been glued to his television for most of the past 24 hours, with only occasional breaks for catnaps, bathroom breaks, and food deliveries. And updates from his partner, Michelle Humphrey.

For he was on forced vacation.

What an idiotic rule!

He had too many accumulated vacation days, and his boss had forced him to take a week off to burn the excess.

"Policy."

"It's a bullshit policy."

"I agree."

"Then why are you making me take them?"

"Because it's policy, and I have no choice but to follow policy."

Reading had slammed a fist on her desk. "If I ever get promoted to a position where I have to follow policy, shoot me."

She had laughed. "Hugh, I don't think you ever have to worry about that."

It had taken him aback for a moment, slightly hurt she felt he would never be worthy of promotion, then he had remembered he didn't give a shit. He was filling his time with something to do in his final years before he'd be put out of the game permanently.

And now, policy had him on a couch, watching the news reports about the unfolding aftermath of the poisoning in Salisbury.

What I would give to be on the ground for this one.

He had left Scotland Yard several years ago after an incident with those Triarii bastards that had made his face a little too public for his bosses' liking, so he had taken the job offer at Interpol to at least stay in the game.

And had regretted it since.

Though he had no choice, if he rationally thought about it.

He just missed the game.

He missed Martin.

He sighed, his eyes drifting up to the heavens.

Why, God, did you have to take him?

His chest tightened, and the too frequent burn threatened to overwhelm him once again. It had been a couple of years, but he still wasn't over the death of his best friend and partner. And he wasn't sure he ever would be.

Thank God for Jim.

James Acton was his best friend now, despite the fact they lived on opposite sides of the pond. They saw each other fairly frequently, however, and often spoke, thanks to his wife's incredible wealth inherited from her late brother, an Internet tycoon who had sold his company before things went bust.

I wonder what Jim would think of this.

Acton was always one for a good conspiracy theory, and right now, the prevailing one among the news channels' talking heads was that it was the Russian government behind it.

And he had to agree.

Initial testing suggested it was a nerve agent, and you couldn't whip that together in the average jihadi apartment. No, this was something different. These people were targeted, or at least one of them was. Everyone else sick were first responders who were obviously exposed after the fact.

According to the update sent to him by his partner, the victims had been identified as Igor and Anna Kulick. Kulick was Russian, now a British citizen, as was his daughter. His wife was deceased, and he lived alone in his small house where they had been found. There was little on his background, though apparently there was a code on the file that the mere viewing of it triggered both MI5 and MI6 alerts, Michelle already receiving visits.

If Kulick was of interest to them, and for both agencies wanting to be notified of anyone looking into him, he clearly was, it suggested he was a former spy, or perhaps even an active one. MI5 handled domestic operations, MI6 foreign, and that meant trouble.

It has to be the Russians.

His phone vibrated on the tabletop and he flinched before grabbing it.

Jim?

He smiled, swiping his thumb. "Hey, Jim, to what do I owe the pleasure?"

"I wish it was a personal call, but something's come up. Something, umm, weird."

Reading frowned, muting his television. Acton and his wife had a propensity for getting themselves into terrifying situations, and too often needed his help to bail them out. But they had returned the favor on more than one occasion, and he would never turn his back on a friend, especially a close one. "What have you got yourselves into this time?"

Acton chuckled. "Hey, this time it has absolutely nothing to do with me, with Laura, or, I *think*, with anyone we know."

Reading's eyes narrowed as he reached for his notebook, flipping it open to a fresh page and readying his pen. "Thank God for small miracles. If you're not up to your neck in it, then who is?"

"A friend of ours came and asked me to call you. He needs a favor."

Reading flipped through the narrow list of mutual friends then stopped. And his heart hammered a little quicker at the implications if he were right, his eyes drifting to the television still showing the unfolding events in the country he called home. "If it's who I'm thinking of, why didn't he contact me himself?"

"This is off-the-books. They need someone on the ground in the UK, outside of the normal loop."

Reading leaned back in his chair, his lips pursed. "So, they don't know who they can trust."

"That's the impression I got."

"Okay, what does he need me to do?"

"Listen, Hugh, it could be dangerous."

Reading grunted. "No more dangerous than anything you two put me through too many times each year."

Acton laughed. "We are rather prolific in our travails, aren't we?"

"Indeed."

"He said if you were willing, contact him through the app on your phone, and he'll send you the details."

Reading gripped the phone in question a little tighter. "I'll do it as soon as I hang up." He drew a deep breath. "So, when am I going to see you two again?"

"Hopefully soon. Laura is heading for London in a couple of weeks, so I'm sure at least you two will tag up. Me, I'm not so sure, but if you want, I could create an international incident somehow and call you for help. Only if you're lonely."

"Bugger off."

Acton roared with laughter. "Listen, gotta go, we have company. Let me know how it works out."

"Will do. Take care of yourself."

"You too." Acton became serious. "I mean it. I got the sense our friend was nervous."

Reading frowned. "If you can't trust your own people, then I don't blame him. Talk to you soon."

He ended the call and activated the secure app Kane had given him if he needed to contact him. He entered his unique code then thumbprint, then typed a quick message.

I'm in.

Then waited, wondering what he had gotten himself into that a CIA spy couldn't trust his own agency with.

Approaching Alex West Residence

Black Forest, Germany

"What's the drone showing?"

"A bunch of pretty trees?"

Kane chuckled at Tommy Granger's response. According to Leroux, the kid was working out well, requiring little guidance on how to work the equipment, and surprisingly good at hacking databases, both foreign and domestic.

Yet he needed more.

"What about infrared?"

"I'm showing several heat sources that appear artificial. No signs of life, but we wouldn't be able to see those inside regardless. That's just in the movies."

There are ways.

"Okay, I'm heading in. Let's just hope by showing up unannounced he doesn't blow my head off."

"Do you think he might?" Tommy sounded genuinely concerned.

And rightly so.

Alex West was a former CIA "super spy," retired for decades, and paranoid for good reason, though with each passing year, more of the enemies he had made serving his country probably passed, making his life a little safer.

He lived on a small plot of land tucked into the Black Forest of southwestern Germany, his nearest neighbor nowhere in sight or earshot, with a canopy of trees blocking any aerial view of his property. Kane had little doubt the place was teeming with protective measures, though none had been evident the first time he had visited the man, "lured" there by the Gray Network.

But that time he had been expected.

This time?

Kane's phone vibrated with a text message. He glanced at it and shook his head, a slight smile breaking out.

Please don't keep me waiting. AW.

"Unbelievable."

"What?" asked Leroux over the comms.

"I just got a text message from West, inviting me in."

"How the hell did he know you were there?"

Kane shrugged as he put the car in gear and pulled away from the side of the road where he had been waiting for the go ahead. "He must have surveillance set up on all the roads leading into the area. Perhaps linked into a facial recognition database that flags any possible threat."

"That's how I'd do it," said Tommy. "Impressive for an old dude to know how to do that."

"I'm more interested in how he got your number," said Leroux.

Kane tossed his phone on the passenger seat as he accelerated. "Someone in the Gray Network, I guess. We obviously have a mole."

"Is it a mole if they're on your side?" asked Tommy.

Kane grunted. "Good question. I have a feeling, however, that West knows exactly what's going on. If people from 1988 are being targeted, and he was there, then he knows he's probably on someone's list, and so is the Chief. He probably put word out to watch the Chief and found out he met with us." Kane turned onto a barely visible dirt road then shook his head as he checked his rearview mirror, a row of bushes sliding back into position, hiding the entrance from the road.

That's new.

Or at least he hadn't noticed it the last time.

He followed the winding path and eventually found the property, parking beside a Volkswagen SUV. He climbed out of his vehicle and approached the front porch. "I'm heading inside now."

But there was no response from Leroux or the team providing him with support, no matter how remote.

"Anyone there?"

"Don't bother. I'm jamming them."

Kane spun toward the gravelly yet strong voice and smiled at Alex West as he emerged from a small shed nestled among the trees. "Alex. You startled me."

"Glad to know I can still sneak up on a trained agent." He eyed Kane. "Or perhaps our agents aren't as good as they once were."

Kane chuckled, extending a hand that was firmly shook. "You look well."

"And I feel well, though these old bones are creaking a little more each day, it seems." He held out a hand, directing Kane into the small home. Kane opened the door and entered, a smile breaking out at the sight.

"I sense a bit more of a feminine touch than last time."

West grunted. "A man gets used to living a certain way for the better part of thirty years, and one woman sweeps in and wants to change everything." He held up a bottle. "Scotch?"

"Absolutely."

Two were poured and they both sat.

"So, where is Adelle?"

"She's visiting our daughter. I was supposed to go, but with recent events, I thought it best I stay away from them."

Kane took a sip of the scotch, the bite swift and welcome. He leaned back in the chair, and noticed a picture on the fireplace mantle of West and his long lost love, Adelle, reunited only a few years ago, and their daughter, a daughter conceived when they were both spies during the Cold War, a daughter he had no idea existed until their reunion.

Kane was happy for the man, and wondered if that would be him and Fang someday, decades from now, with grown children and a happy, comfortable home.

Only if you survive the job.

"So, you knew I was coming."

"Of course."

"I won't bother asking how. Why don't you tell me what you know? I have a feeling it's more than I do."

West chuckled, swirling his scotch. "Why don't you tell me what your boss told you?"

Kane nodded. "Very well. All I know is that in 1988 there was an assassination attempt on Gorbachev. It looks like both Soviets and Americans were involved, and that you saved the day, and my boss' life."

"And that's all you know?"

"From what happened then? Yes. Today, we have the Chief's Soviet counterpart poisoned, along with his daughter, and all signs point to the Russian government being behind it."

West took a drink. "So, you don't know much. Let me fill you in on a few more details. Back in '88, I recognized that things were changing, and that not everyone was happy about it, especially on the Soviet side. I figured there were some that would do anything to stop the changes that Gorbachev was pushing, and once I heard about the summit, I knew if they were going to make their move, it would be then. For months, I had been letting it slip to my contacts on the Soviet side that I wasn't happy with things, and that if peace were to come, I'd be out of a job on some measly pension." He gestured at the walls surrounding them. "Like now."

Kane smiled. "You seem to be doing fine."

West shrugged. "I found a sympathetic ear among a lot of my counterparts, so when a double-agent was looking for someone to supply him with an American sniper rifle, he approached me with an extremely generous offer." He took another sip. "I accepted. I provided the weapon, and knew with the summit only days away, that either Reagan or Gorbachev was the target. Which one didn't really matter. Either one could lead to war, and would definitely end any hopes of peace for another generation."

"So, you supplied the weapon. Then what?"

"I told my guy I wanted in. I told him I was already assigned to the security detail, which was easy enough to arrange through Langley, and would be able to override the comms until the shot was taken. It was obvious they were trying to frame our side by using one of our own weapons, so I pushed the idea that manipulating our own comms would make it look like a rogue operation from our side."

"It obviously worked."

"Brilliantly. I was called the next day and taken to a briefing where the entire plot was laid out by a man I now know was named Yury Minkin."

"You identified him after the fact?"

West nodded. "*Well* after. Three weeks ago, in fact."

Kane's eyebrows shot up. "Excuse me?"

"He's one of the richest men in Russia. A defense contractor. He was just arrested by the Russian government on fraud charges."

Kane's head bobbed as he recalled reading about it. The charges were thought to be bullshit, trumped-up accusations meant to embarrass a man the Kremlin feared had ambitions to the throne. "Why do *you* think he was arrested?"

"I have no proof of this, mind you, but did you know that one of his company's projects is to catalog and destroy much of Russia's chemical and biological weapons stockpile?"

Kane's eyes widened slightly as he realized where West was going with this. "Let me guess. Part of that stockpile includes Novichok-type weapons?"

"Exactly. My guess is that either he supplied the nerve agent used in the attack in Salisbury two days ago, or he's going to be framed for it if it becomes necessary."

Kane blasted a breath through his lips. "So, if he supplied the nerve agent, then he's involved in the attempt on Kulick's life, and if he didn't, then whoever is trying to frame him, is, and if that's the case, then the Russian government definitely is involved."

West wagged a finger. "Not necessarily. It could be that someone is trying to make it look like the Kremlin is involved. Remember, Minkin was arrested three weeks ago on fraud charges. It's conceivable that he was set up for these lesser charges, and the Kremlin are just patsies here."

Kane frowned. "Given their track record, I find that highly unlikely."

"Agreed. That country is quickly devolving back into the Soviet Union, just by a different name."

"Just give him a few more years."

West chuckled. "I see you're a cynic like me. Good. It'll help you live longer, perhaps long enough to grow old with that beautiful young woman you're now living with."

Kane's eyebrows rose slightly. "You've been keeping tabs on me."

"I have." West waved his hand, dismissing the tangent. "So, once they knew what I could offer, I was in, and taken to this briefing. There were only six men in the room. I was one of them, so was Minkin, and so was the shooter, though I don't know his name. One was killed at the side entrance to the building, along with his American assigned counterpart who wasn't in the room nor part of the plan. The Russian was the one who let Boykov in for the shot, and provided him with the key to access the top floor."

"Who killed them?"

"Probably Boykov, perhaps under supplementary orders that were given after the initial briefing. The target was never mentioned specifically in the meeting, yet he knew who he was supposed to shoot, which means he was given further instructions after the fact. There were two other men who, like the rest of us, said nothing. I assume they were Russian, but can't be positive. I found no evidence of American involvement beyond what I did. There's a very good chance they're dead by now, but we can't be sure."

"Do you think one of them is behind this?"

West shrugged. "It's possible. I think we can rule out Minkin, obviously, and myself"—he flashed a smile—"and the dead guy at the door. I shot Boykov, which leaves two others. And, of course, we don't know who else was involved beyond that room."

"But why now? What's changed that thirty years after the fact, they want to kill those involved in a failed assassination plot?"

West shook his head. "It could be anything, but my guess is someone is going to make a play for power, and they don't want anyone being able to point at them as having been involved."

Kane chewed his cheek as he processed this new information. The good news was that there wasn't American involvement in the plot as Morrison had feared. West was the one responsible for hijacking their frequencies. But they were no closer to discovering who was behind everything than when he left for Germany. "We need more to go on."

"I think you know who you need to contact."

Kane nodded. "Viktor Zorkin."

"Exactly."

"He's dropped off the radar. No one knows how to reach him. In fact, Langley's not even sure if he's still alive."

"He is." West finished his drink. "In fact, I contacted him three weeks ago, as soon as I recognized Minkin on the news. He's expecting you."

Kane grunted. "You never cease to impress."

West pointed at an envelope sitting on the table between them. "Your travel documents are inside, including a Russian visa, and everything you need to know." He rose, extending a hand. "Good luck, my boy. I think you're going to need it on this one."

Pechatniki Pre-trial Detention Center

Moscow, Russia

Boykov's entire body ached, and he cursed his old age. It wasn't as if having an entire apartment building collapse under younger feet wouldn't have resulted in a few scrapes and bruises, it was that he could have tolerated the pain and pushed through it a little easier.

Instead, he had self-medicated with a little more vodka than usual, and spent a few hours on and off in an ice bath at the fleabag hotel on the opposite side of the city he normally haunted.

He was feeling much better this evening than he had two nights ago.

And he was in a relatively good mood for someone with a price on his head.

The newscasts were blaming Jihadists for the attack, and he wasn't surprised. It was certainly their modus operandi. A van, packed with explosives, had been parked in front of the building and detonated remotely, blowing out the ground level, bringing everything above it down like a controlled detonation.

And that was why he had survived.

They overachieved.

Less explosives would have blown out only a portion of the main floor, causing the building to topple, slamming his upper floor onto the street below. Instead, he dropped, a floor at a time, stacking on the one below, minimizing the force, but crushing to death most under him.

It was the upper floor apartment that had saved him, and he'd never curse it again when the elevator wasn't working.

He grunted.

There's nothing to go back to, so that won't be a problem.

He checked his watch and inhaled slowly. What he was about to do was stupid, but with a price on one's head, one was apt to do stupid things. If it got him tossed in prison, then so be it. There were ways to end one's life behind bars should it come to that, for he had no intention of spending his final years confined to a tiny room.

He had done enough of that on the outside.

Today, he was here to try and find out who was behind the attempt on his life, from the only person he could think of who might know.

Yet it all depended on one large assumption that didn't fit what had happened so far. If this was related to the old days and the failed assassination attempt, then why blow up a building and make it look like Islamic terrorists? Why not just put a bullet in his head and be done with it? And the phone call had him confused as well. It was a woman. There were no women involved back then, and none of those involved were the type to use them today. Who was she? Was she behind this, or simply a contractor?

He had to know, and only Minkin might be able to help him.

But would he be willing?

To Minkin, he was the man who had failed. He was the one responsible for everything that had happened afterward.

Yet Minkin had fallen squarely on his feet. If anything, he should be happy that the mission had failed. He was a billionaire because of it.

And then there was the fact Minkin was his estranged brother.

At least that was the line he had fed a drunk guard last night after his shift had ended. He had cased the jail and watched the shift change carefully, ignoring those going home to their families, ignoring the young ones who might still have hope, instead picking out those who were older, nearing the end of a career with a slashed pension to look forward to and no one to go home to.

Those heading to the bar to drown out their sorrows.

Those with shattered dreams, where one spark of hope, no matter how remote, might allow themselves to be used.

"Tough day?"

The man's name had been Moriz, overheard as the busty waitress in a too-short skirt served him his usual. Boykov had sent him a drink when his first was getting low, under the pretense of having himself once been on the job.

The glass was hoisted in thanks, and a kindly wave to join him given.

He was in.

And after several hours of drinking with Moriz Grekov, of exchanging war stories and how the Kremlin's new pension policies were killing him, and would soon doom his new friend to a horribly meager retirement, he had told him his own troubles of dying from colon cancer, and wishing to see his brother one last time.

"But he won't see me. He's ashamed of his older brother."

"Why?"

"I was a drunk, and ungrateful, I guess. To be honest, I was jealous of his success. I served my country for decades and got nothing after the collapse, and what happened to him? He became rich!"

Grekov growled. "Too many of those bastards got rich off our backs. It was all who you knew back then."

Boykov spat. "Still is."

Grekov's head bobbed. "Tell me about it. We've got one of those assholes in my jail right now. You should see how he's getting treated! It's infuriating."

"It is, but blood is blood. He's my younger brother, and I don't have much time left. I want to see him one last time, just to say I'm sorry, and to, you know, say I love him. Our poor mother, God rest her soul, wouldn't want me leaving this earth without first patching things up between the two of us."

A tear rolled down Grekov's cheek. "I lost my wife five years ago. Still miss her."

"Do you have any brothers or sisters?"

Grekov sighed. "One brother, but he lives in America, the lucky bastard."

"At least you have time to see him." He slapped him on the shoulder. "You should. Soon."

Grekov grunted. "With what money?" He drained his vodka, flagging the waitress down for two more. "Now what about you? You should see your brother. Demand to see him if he says no."

Boykov frowned, shaking his head. "Unfortunately, it's not that easy."

"Why not?"

"Well, you're not going to believe this, and I didn't realize it until we started talking, but that bastard you've got locked up in your jail, is my brother."

Grekov's jaw dropped, as well as a bit of drool. "You're kidding me! What are the chances?"

Apparently very good, if it's a drunk crunching the numbers.

"I know, right! And that's the problem. He's behind bars, and if I ask to see him, he'll just say no. He'll never give me the chance, and it's not like I can just stay there and demand to see him. Your buddies are liable to have me arrested!"

Grekov snorted. "Maybe I can have them put you in the next cell so he'll be forced to talk to you!"

They both roared in laughter, Boykov slapping him on the back. "That's not a bad idea, my friend, not a bad idea at all! And if I can bury the hatchet with my brother, maybe he'd be grateful and share some of those billions with the man responsible." He gave him a shoulder shake. "You!"

They both paused, Grekov's drunken mind spinning, Boykov waiting for him to come up with the idea for himself. "Saay, *that's* not a half-bad idea, my friend." Grekov lowered his voice. "Do you think he might?"

"Might what?"

"Be grateful, you know, share a few rubles with the man who helped reunite him with his long lost brother."

Boykov stared at him for a moment, pausing for effect, then nodded. "I think he absolutely would. My brother is a very generous man. Our falling out wasn't about him not giving me money, it was about me being a jerk about it, then telling him to go shove it where the sun didn't shine." Boykov leaned back, shaking a finger. "I think you're onto something, here, my friend." He quickly leaned back in, lowering his voice. "We might be able to help each other. If you could get me in to see my brother, and I can patch things up with him, to say one last goodbye, I'll make sure he takes care of you so you don't have to worry about that crummy pension you're expected to live on for the next twenty years."

A smile spread across Grekov's face. "I think I like the sound of that."

"Then how do we do it?"

"When my shift starts tomorrow, I'll have him transferred into a private meeting room, one they use to meet with their lawyers, so no cameras, and then let you in the back service entrance. It's barely twenty meters from the room. I can probably give you about thirty minutes alone with him. When you're done, just text my cellphone, and I'll come let you out."

Boykov smiled broadly. "You're a good man, my friend, a good man. I feel good about this. I think my brother won't have a choice but to hear me out, and I'm sure he'll forgive me, and be *very* grateful."

Grekov raised his vodka. "Let's hope you're right!"

And let's hope you remember all this tomorrow.

And he had.

After soothing himself in an ice bath, then getting as much sleep as he could manage, Grekov had texted him.

Are we still on?

His reply had been swift.

Absolutely.

A few details had been exchanged, along with reassurances of a potentially huge payout that would allow the poor man to retire in comfort, and the rendezvous was set.

Boykov checked his watch, the expected text from Grekov late.

He frowned.

Cold feet? Second thoughts?

It could be anything. He had watched Grekov enter the jail on time, though he did look a little worse for wear, their drinking perhaps a little more than the disillusioned man was used to. He was inside, and any number of things could have delayed him.

His phone vibrated, a burner he had picked up shortly after the explosion.

He smiled.

Now.

He rose from the bench he had been sitting on for the past half hour, and strode across the street with purpose, heading directly for the back service entrance, unguarded, the door only operable from the inside, a security camera mounted nearby with a clear view of anyone approaching.

He did nothing to hide himself.

For he wasn't a wanted man.

Not by the authorities.

Not yet.

The door opened as he neared, and Grekov beckoned him inside. Boykov smiled broadly, jogging the last few steps. "I was beginning to get worried."

Grekov closed the door. "It took me a little longer to get your brother to the interrogation room than I expected. Sorry." He paused. "You think…"

Boykov slapped him on the back. "I *know* this is going to work. We're both going to get what we want out of this."

Grekov smiled. "Then let's do this." He pointed down the long, windowless corridor. "Third door on the right. Text me when you're done. It should only take me a few minutes to get to you. No matter what you do, don't leave the room without me."

"Got it."

He followed Grekov to the door and drew a deep breath, wondering what sort of greeting he would get, and hoping it was delayed enough for Grekov to hear none of it.

Grekov pushed the door open. "You've got a visitor."

Boykov stepped into the room, smiling broadly, but saying nothing, instead turning to give Grekov a wink and push the door closed.

"Good luck!" whispered Grekov.

"To both of us."

The door shut and Boykov turned to face Minkin, a blank stare on the man's face.

"Who the hell are you?"

Boykov sat across from him, the room empty save the bolted down table and two chairs. "My name is Vasily Boykov. Do you recognize it?"

Minkin stared at him, no sign of recognition there for a few moments, then suddenly his eyes widened. "No, I don't, but I recognize your face." He lowered his voice. "You were there that day!"

Boykov nodded. "I was. As were several others."

Minkin glanced around the room, clearly nervous. "Why are you here?"

"First things first. If anyone asks, I'm your long lost brother, Vasily. You haven't seen me in over a decade, and I'm here to patch things up with you before I die of colon cancer."

"Umm, okay?"

"And that guard you just saw? His name is Grekov. If you get out of here, you're going to pay him a handsome reward so he doesn't have to starve on that shit pension he's got to look forward to."

Minkin's eyebrows shot up. "Fine. But I doubt I'm getting out of this. Not with what I've been accused of."

"I thought it was just some trumped up fraud charge."

Minkin shook his head. "Do you really believe everything you see on our state media?"

Boykov grunted, leaning back in his chair. "Not for a second." He pursed his lips. "Which brings us back to why I'm here." He tapped his chin. "And I wonder if it's related."

Minkin's eyes narrowed. "How do you mean?"

"Someone tried to kill me."

"Who?"

"I don't know. I got a phone call from a woman who knew my real name, then a bomb detonated, taking out my entire damned building."

"That thing I saw on the news?"

Boykov eyed him. "You've got access to a television?"

Minkin shrugged. "Being rich does have its perks."

Boykov chuckled. "I wouldn't know."

Minkin regarded him for a moment. "You said a woman called you?"

"Yes." His eyes narrowed. "Why? Is that significant?"

"Perhaps. Perhaps not. But I was visited by a woman only moments before I was arrested, and she tried to kill me as well."

Boykov's eyes shot wide. "That sounds like too much of a coincidence to me. Two people, involved in a plot to assassinate Gorbachev thirty years ago, both targeted within weeks of each other by a woman of all people?"

"I agree."

Boykov scratched his chin. "Who do you think is trying to kill us?"

Minkin regarded him for a moment. "I have my theories, but if you want to hear them, you have to get me out of here."

Boykov laughed. "And just how the hell am I supposed to do that?"

"I have people that will take care of it, but they need to know when, and no one is talking. You need to find out when I'm making my next court appearance. Can you?"

Boykov chewed his cheek for a moment. Grekov should either know or be able to find out. But he'd need an incentive. There was no way he was going to believe that he needed to know the exact time of his "brother's" transfer. "I can, but I'll need to pay off that guard I spoke of."

"Give me something to write on."

Boykov pulled a small notepad and pen from his pocket, sliding it across the table. Minkin jotted down a phone number then two words.

Phoenix Rising.

He pushed the paper and pen back. "Call that number, give them that codeword, and tell them what you need. They'll transfer whatever you want into whatever account you want. Is a million Euros enough?"

Boykov grunted. "It better be."

"And I assume you want to be paid?"

Boykov paused, his eyebrows rising slightly. He hadn't even considered it, though perhaps he too should have a taste. It might help him survive long enough to find out who was trying to kill him. "Of course."

"A million?"

"I like round numbers."

"Very well." Minkin leaned across the table. "But if you take my money and don't come through, you'll wish you had died in that explosion."

Boykov didn't bother faking fear. A man like Minkin would be able to tell. "Don't threaten a man who's already dead. I'll have half transferred to my guy, then when he comes through with the time, the other half. If your people can't get you out, don't blame him. He keeps his money. I'll take my million as soon as he comes through with the time. Same deal. If your people screw it up, that's on them, not me. Agreed?"

Minkin smiled. "I see why they chose you to be the shooter. Nothing bothers you."

Boykov's eyes narrowed. "I thought *you* chose me?"

Minkin laughed, shaking his head. "You and that girl both seem to think I was far more important than I was."

"When you get out, I want to be there so you can tell me everything."

"Just tell my people, and they'll make it happen."

Boykov rose, leaning in on white knuckles. "And if *you* betray me, *you'll* wish you died in prison."

Off-the-books Operations Center

Outside Bethesda, Maryland

Leroux yawned and stretched, looking about the small room to see what had awoken him. Three more gentle taps on the door answered his question.

"Enter."

The door opened and Sonya Tong stepped into the darkness, silhouetted by the light of Kane's private operation. "Sorry to wake you, but we've got some intel that I think you need to see."

Leroux stood, forgetting he wasn't wearing any pants. Sonya quickly turned her head, but not before getting in a good look. "Sorry about that. I'll meet you in ops in a sec."

"Yes, sir."

The door closed, plunging him into complete darkness once again, and he cursed, groping around for his cellphone that he had left on the nightstand. He found it and activated the flashlight then switched on the table lamp.

They were inside two massive, converted shipping containers, buried among hundreds of others, at a storage yard on the outskirts of Bethesda, less than half an hour from Langley. One of the containers was a fully equipped living quarters for four, well stocked with provisions to last months if not longer, the other side jam-packed with a state of the art operations center. Dedicated lines attaching them to the grid and backbone of the Internet gave them access to everything they might need, and Leroux was certain there were also backup generators and satellite access should it become necessary.

Fortunately, Armageddon wasn't knocking on their door just yet.

He quickly dressed then joined Sonya and Tommy in the ops center. "What did you find?"

Tommy pointed at a screen showing a woman stepping out of a van. Leroux's eyes narrowed.

"What am I looking at?"

"Remember that explosion last night in Moscow?"

"Yes. Is that the van they used?"

"Yeah. Somebody just posted this video online and it's going viral. A lot of people are in a huff that Muslims were being blamed without any proof. Looks kinda white, doesn't she?"

Leroux nodded. "Not exactly the Jihadi type."

"Nope."

"Any idea who she is?"

"Not yet, but I'm running her face through my little routine that scours social media for matches. I didn't want to hack into any of the big guys just yet."

"Good thinking. But why do you think she has anything to do with what we're working on?"

Sonya answered his question by bringing up a translated Russian arrest report. "Because of this. Thanks to Kane's meeting with West, we now know Yury Minkin is involved. I started digging into his background, and couldn't find anything extraordinary beyond the fact he was once KGB, then made out big in the carving up of state assets after the collapse of the Soviet Union."

"Which means he must have had something on some powerful people."

Sonya nodded. "Or was owed big time. Until he was arrested three weeks ago on fraud charges, he appeared squeaky clean for the past twenty-plus years. He owns a massive defense contractor, has loads of deals with the Russian government, and was making a killing off their rearmament plans. All until three weeks ago, when everything came tumbling down on him."

"Falling out with the Kremlin?"

"That's what the speculation is, though no one knows quite what it's over. He's never shown any interest in politics, keeps a low profile, rarely gives press interviews, and never comments on domestic matters. Nobody knows why the Kremlin would want to take him down."

Tommy shrugged. "Maybe it *is* just simple fraud?"

Leroux sat. "It could be, but I don't believe in coincidences. According to West, this guy was not only in the room, he was giving the briefing. That means he had to be at or near the top of the conspiracy. He gets arrested, three weeks later there's an attempted poisoning using nerve agents that his company has access to, of a man who wasn't in the room but had seen the assassin." He turned to Sonya. "So, what's the connection between this woman and Minkin?"

"I'm not sure yet, but when Minkin was arrested, there was a separate report filed then retracted, that they were looking for a woman that matches her description. It could be just coincidence, but I know how you feel about them."

"Okay, let's start pulling surveillance footage from the day of the arrest, see if we can spot anything. If we can put the same woman in both locations, then we know she's involved."

Tommy cracked his knuckles. "Just let me work my magic."

Salisbury District Hospital

Salisbury, United Kingdom

Interpol Agent Hugh Reading, on vacation, stood outside the isolation ward holding the poison victims. The emergency personnel had minor exposure, with most expected to recover fully over the coming days, but the father and daughter were something different. They were knocking on death's door, and their survival was doubtful.

Nobody knew who they were beyond their basic identities, though Reading knew more. He was privy to the fact this man used to be KGB, and that he had been partnered with Director Morrison of the CIA in 1988.

And that he had recognized a man who would later attempt to assassinate Gorbachev, and fail.

He was certain the two events were connected, only by the fact of the method used in the murder attempt. Novichok was only available to the Russians and no one else. And it wasn't exactly lying around at every military installation for someone to steal. It was all located in Shikhany, a highly secure facility.

No, the Russians were behind this. The questions were why, and how to prove it.

Yet for the moment, it appeared there would be no getting close to the only people who might know, despite his credentials. Not only were they both unconscious, they were behind a wall of security.

"Hugh?"

Reading spun on his heel and did a doubletake as he recognized an old colleague. "DI Nelson? My word, I haven't seen you in years!"

Nelson extended a hand, giving him a hearty handshake. "Not since you left the Yard and joined Interpol." He bowed slightly. "And it's Detective *Chief* Inspector now."

Reading smiled broadly, his prediction that the young man would achieve big things confirmed. "Congratulations." He jerked his thumb over his shoulder at the circus behind him, a way in perhaps having just presented itself. "You involved in this?"

Nelson nodded. "I am. My promotion meant moving here. Quite the thing, quite the thing. These damned Russians need to be put on a leash."

"So, you think it's the Russians?"

Nelson eyed him. "Don't you? I mean, who else could it be?"

"Oh, I think so too, I'm just happy to hear I'm not off base." He lowered his voice. "Any leads? Any idea who actually did the deed?"

"We're canvassing, of course, interviewing all the neighbors, pulling all the CCTV footage, but get this." He leaned in, lowering his voice. "We think it might have been a woman."

Reading's eyebrows shot up. "A woman?"

"Yes. We have footage showing her walking up to their door, doing something that we can't see because her body blocks the camera, then walk away. The victim even held the gate open for her!"

"So, she must have been waiting for them, saw them coming, planted the nerve agent, then left." He paused, his jaw dropping slowly. "It was the door handle, wasn't it?"

Nelson slapped him on the shoulder. "You've still got it. That's exactly right. They both touched it when they went inside, then some of the first responders did as well, though most of it had already transferred to the intended targets."

"We don't think the daughter was intentionally targeted, do we?"

Nelson shrugged. "I think there was a message being sent here. It's his residence, so he was definitely the target, and taking out the daughter was probably a nice bonus for them."

"Will they survive?"

Nelson frowned. "The daughter managed to dial 9-9-9 before passing out, so first responders got there very quickly. If not, they likely would have been found when the neighbors started complaining about the smell. The doctors are saying it's fifty-fifty right now, though we're not letting the press know that. We want whoever is behind this to think they've succeeded and it's just a matter of time."

Reading extended his hand and Nelson took it. "It was great seeing you again. Do you mind if I give you a call for an update?"

"Not at all." Nelson fished a business card from his pocket. "Just in case you lost my number." He winked.

Reading laughed. "It really was good to see you."

Nelson became serious. "Listen, I was sorry to hear about Martin. A great loss."

Reading's good mood disappeared at the mention of his late partner. "It was a shock, to say the least."

Nelson forced a smile. "I'll tell you what. When this is over, we'll get some of the lads together for some drinks, and we'll hoist a few in his memory."

Reading smiled, thrilled with the idea. "I'll hold you to it."

He headed for the nurses' station, his heart aching at the mention of his former partner, seeing Nelson for the first time in years causing too many memories to flood back. He missed Chaney desperately, his mourning for his friend's loss never really ending, not a day going by without some sort of emotional reaction, though there was a little more laughter than tears now.

But all that would have to wait. He had a job to do, and thanks to Nelson, might now have a solid lead.

Now, where are you, Nurse Midge Aldrin?

Off-the-books Operations Center

Outside Bethesda, Maryland

Leroux paced the length of the shipping container, the claustrophobia getting to him. He hadn't seen the light of day since setting foot inside, nor taken a breath of fresh air. When Kane had given him the address, he had been stunned at what he found, and realized just how prepared Kane was for any eventuality.

His friend trusted no one.

Well, almost no one. He assumed Kane trusted what he thought of as the inner circle. Himself and Sherrie, as well as Fang, and perhaps even Morrison, though their boss was bound by orders from above that might leave Kane twisting in the wind should the Administration decide he no longer served their purposes.

Leroux regarded the equipment surrounding him, now manned by a yawning Sonya, and an eager Tommy who seemed filled with boundless energy.

Reminds me of my Red Bull days.

He had been addicted to the stuff, the caffeine-infused beverage fueling late nights behind the keyboard, until Sherrie had finally convinced him to give it up. She had been the incentive he had been searching for, and once found, going cold turkey had been difficult, yet successful, and now he no longer missed the addictive concoction.

Though in times like these, he sometimes wished he could indulge.

Sonya yawned again.

"Why don't you take a nap?"

She shook her head. "I'll be fine."

"No, that's an order. Grab a few hours. You'll be that much sharper."

She sighed, her shoulders slumping. "You're right." She rose, heading for the doorway that connected them to the second container. She turned. "Wake me if you need me."

He nodded and she disappeared. His eyes lingered after her, and he wondered what might have happened between them if Sherrie hadn't entered his life when she did. If they hadn't met, or hadn't made things work, would he have had the courage to ask Sonya out? She liked him, there was no doubt of that, but if it weren't for Sherrie, he would still be that puniest of men he once was, with zero self-confidence, and absolutely no skills when it came to women.

Today, the way he was now, if he were single and Sonya didn't report to him, he could see himself asking her out, though the very thought of it sent butterflies rippling through his stomach, then a wave of guilt at the thought. But the man he was before?

Never in a million years would he have found the courage to ask her.

"Got something."

Leroux tore his eyes away from the closed door and took a seat beside Tommy, the young man proving to be an extremely valuable addition to their unofficial team. If it weren't for his history, he might make a good formal addition.

I'll have to talk to the Chief when this is all done.

"What have you got?"

"I found the woman Agent Reading told us about." He pointed at a screen showing footage of a woman walking up to the victim's door, standing there for several seconds, then leaving, the gate to the row of houses opened by the victim himself.

"You can't really see her face there, can you?"

Tommy shook his head. "Nope. But you can on this one."

Another video displayed, the same woman walking quickly down the street then climbing into a car, but not before she took a glance over her shoulder, her face revealed to the camera. "Can you plot that?"

"Already done."

Leroux's heart hammered at the anticipation in Tommy's voice. "And?"

"And she's an exact match for the woman in Moscow who planted the bomb the next day."

Leroux slapped Tommy on the back. "Excellent work! Do we have the list of residents yet?"

"Yes, it arrived when you were asleep. Sonya is running it against our databases, so hopefully, if there's something to find, we'll know soon."

"And that tip from Special Agent West about the woman possibly involved in the Minkin arrest? Anything yet?"

"No, but it's just a matter of time. Everyone is on social media these days, whether they want to be or not."

"Okay. Let's track this woman in Salisbury. See if we can find out where she went."

"Won't the Brits be doing that anyway?"

Leroux nodded. "Yes, but they're not likely to share what they find with us, and we need to know where she is. Right now, it looks like she's involved with two serious attacks in as many days. We need to figure out who she is, and where she is, so we can stop her, find out who she's working for, and why, so we can prevent the Chief from becoming a target."

"Roger Roger. I'll find her for you, that's a promise."

Leroux ignored the overconfidence, though from what he had seen so far, the kid might just have the skills to come through.

It was a good team.

Sonya was a fantastic analyst, one he had come to rely on over the years. Her recognizing the fact that a suspected Islamic terrorist bombing in Moscow of an apartment building, actually carried out by a blond white woman, might be related to the woman the police had sought when Minkin was arrested, was brilliant, and had proven correct now that they had matched her to the Salisbury attack.

This woman was the key, and now that they had clear images of her face, it was only a matter of time before they found her.

The world was wired.

And he had access to almost all the cameras out there.

Sooner or later, she'd cross paths with one of them.

Podzemnyy Parking Garage

Moscow, Russia

A match struck to Kane's right and he smiled at the familiar face revealed by the flare. The cigarette lit, the man's footsteps echoed in the parking garage as he emerged from the darkness.

"Special Agent Kane. Good to see you again."

Kane shook the man's hand. "Viktor Zorkin, I'm glad to see you're still alive. I wasn't so sure."

"What is it they say? Rumors of my death have been greatly exaggerated?"

Kane chuckled. "Something like that." Viktor Zorkin had been KGB during the height of the Cold War, a master spy and rival to Alex West, though one who always was guided by honor, rather than dogma. Kane had worked with him before, and trusted him not only because the man had Alex West's blessing, but because he had been in enough scraps with him to know whose side he was on. He glanced around the rundown structure. "Are we secure here?"

"Secure enough. None of the cameras actually work here, at least for the moment." He beckoned Kane toward a nearby car and popped the trunk, revealing two duffel bags. "Everything a good spy needs to start a small war."

Kane unzipped the bags, making a quick inspection, then closed them back up. "And the car?" He stepped back to make sure it wasn't a certain British sportscar.

"Clean. No one will pull you over for expired tags or a broken taillight."

"Excellent." He turned to Zorkin. "So, is there anything you can tell me? We've got six suspects."

Zorkin shook his head. "No, you've got far more than six."

Kane's eyebrows shot up, only joking about the six since one of them was West, Zorkin's rival during the Cold War but a friend in the years that ensued, another was killed the day of the assassination by the shooter, and the shooter was left for dead by West. "Am I missing something? We have West, Minkin who West confirmed was in the room, the shooter whom West killed, the man at the entrance who was killed with his American counterpart, and two others. That leaves only those two that might be alive that could be suspects."

"All men too old to be rushing off to England to poison people, don't you think?"

Kane regarded Zorkin. "I've seen you in action, and you fit the age group."

Zorkin chuckled. "True, my friend, but I think we need to widen the suspect pool a bit."

"To whom?"

"Family, friends, sons, daughters. All I'm saying is, don't put your blinders on so quickly."

"Daughters." Kane pursed his lips. "Funny you should mention that. We've got a blond woman linked to the poisoning in Salisbury, an explosion at a building in Moscow, and possibly to the arrest of Minkin."

Zorkin's eyebrows shot up. "Really?"

Kane nodded. "I'm surprised you weren't already aware."

Zorkin grunted. "It's getting harder to be kept in the loop as the years pass. Too many old friends dying of natural causes. And some unnatural." His eyes narrowed. "One of the two other men must have been the target. Do you have a list of names for that explosion?"

Kane pulled out his phone, bringing up the list of residents that Leroux had sent him. He handed it over and Zorkin quickly scrolled through before his eyes flared. "Luka Yerkhov. I know this name."

Kane's pulse picked up a few beats. "From where?"

"The old days. But why do I remember it?" He leaned against the car, scratching at his leathery skin, then smiled. "That crafty bastard!"

"What?"

"Luka Yerkhov was an alias used by none other than our shooter, Vasily Boykov."

Trepidation swept over Kane, his voice lowering. "That means West didn't kill him." A pit formed in his stomach as he wondered for a moment whether West had lied.

"Interesting. It's not like my old adversary to fail, though his job was to foil the assassination, which he did." He eyed Kane for a moment. "You think he might be involved."

It was a statement, not a question, yet Kane answered regardless. "The thought had crossed my mind."

Zorkin chuckled. "Then put your mind at ease. There's no way Alex West was involved in this. I assume Director Morrison told you what happened?"

"Yes. West tricked Boykov, shot him in the back, then told Morrison to get lost."

"Exactly. If he were involved, don't you think he would have killed your boss as well?"

Kane nodded. "True. Let's assume West is innocent. It just makes things simpler. I'm going to get my people on Boykov and see if he was killed in the bombing. I like your idea of a relation being involved. She could be the daughter of one of the two men we don't know."

"Or the man who was killed the day of, or of Boykov, or of someone else we don't know about. We can't know."

"True. But at least we have another lead thanks to that memory of yours." Kane chewed his cheek. "But where to start?"

"Minkin was in the room. We know that from Alex. A blond woman was momentarily wanted after his arrest. That suggests she was either there to perhaps kill him, or is related to him."

"Or was buying the nerve agent from him."

Zorkin cursed. "My memory might be good, but my ability to sense conspiracies is fading. You're right of course, that's exactly it. His company could have access to that. She meets him, makes the purchase, then he gets raided. She escapes somehow, someone remembers seeing her, perhaps a secretary, they try to find her, but someone quashes it." He smiled. "If I were you, I'd try to find out who killed the bulletin on this woman. It might lead to who is behind this."

"You think someone is protecting her?"

"We have to assume she's a nobody. If you've linked her to at least two events, then so have the authorities, and if they've identified her, she'd be all over the news by now."

Kane grunted. "And nobodies don't have the money or connections to buy Novichok nerve agents, or explosives to fill a van."

"Exactly. She's being protected, and probably funded, by someone of means with connections. *Good* connections. You need to find out why this woman was wanted at the time of the arrest. In fact, forget who canceled the search. He'll have had some underling do it, or have made a phone call that there will be no record of, and denied by whoever received it." Zorkin wagged his finger. "No, you need to find out who Minkin sold the Novichok to."

Kane frowned. "Obviously, but how do I do that?"

Zorkin smiled. "What does every powerful executive have?"

Kane shrugged. "A fatter wallet than me?"

Zorkin chuckled. "That, and a secretary he's banging."

Off-the-books Operations Center

Outside Bethesda, Maryland

"Her name is Svetlana Lobanov. She's a former swimsuit model, graced the covers of a bunch of Russian magazines before those same magazines started reporting she was having an affair with Yury Minkin, which he denied and sued them for libel."

Sonya stared at the photos of the busty blonde flashing across one of the displays. "Did he win?"

Tommy continued scanning his notes. "It looks like things were settled out of court, no new photos or articles appeared, and the story's gone cold for the past two years."

Leroux stretched, fighting a yawn. "And this is his secretary now?"

"Yup."

Sonya grunted. "I wonder what the wife thinks of that."

"Nothing. She died six months ago."

"It probably killed her knowing this bitch was working twenty feet from her husband day in and day out."

Leroux tore his eyes away from the chesty photos. "Do we have a location on her?"

"No, but I have an address for her. It's a high-end condo in Moscow."

Sonya shook her head. "No doubt paid for by her boss." She sighed. "Sometimes I wished I looked like that so I wouldn't have to work for anything."

Tommy spun toward her. "Are you kidding? You're the bomb! You're way better looking than her. Everything about her is fake. You're real. That's way more attractive."

Sonya blushed and Leroux smiled slightly, letting her enjoy the flattery for a few moments before yanking his "team" back on track. "Okay, get that address to Dylan and any details you think might be relevant."

Tommy tapped a few keys. "Done."

"Any luck with the traces of our other blonde?"

Sonya nodded, bringing up some footage playing out in sequence showing their suspect. "We've got her arriving in London the day before, picking up a rental car, staying at her hotel overnight, then arriving in Salisbury and parking near the victim's house. She watches them leave, waits for quite a few hours before we see our victims returning, she goes ahead, plants the nerve agent, leaves, exchanges pleasantries with the man she's trying to murder, gets in her car, heads to London, gets on a plane for Moscow, and is out of British airspace before anyone knows the seriousness of the situation. She's back in Moscow where the next evening she blows up a building, killing dozens."

"Cold," muttered Tommy, clearly disturbed.

Leroux regarded him. "You okay?"

Tommy shrugged. "Yeah, it's just, well, hard to believe there are people out there that are so evil, you know?"

Sonya turned her chair to face him, still blushing slightly at his impassioned defense of her beauty. "You sort of get used to it over time. You just have to realize that it's our job to try and stop them, and more often than not we do."

"But you hear about terrorist attacks all the time!"

Leroux nodded. "Yes, but you almost never hear about the ones we stop. If the public knew how many terrorist attacks were actually attempted and stopped, they'd be terrified. There's been over one-hundred serious attacks stopped by people like us since Nine-Eleven. And that's just on home soil. There's been hundreds if not thousands more worldwide that have been stopped thanks to our efforts and those of our allies."

"But what about Europe? You hear about attacks there all the time." Tommy jabbed a finger at the monitors without looking. "And I read about what's really happening, that the press and the governments over there are covering up. It's insane!"

Leroux grunted. "Unfortunately, Europe is pretty much lost already. You can't let millions of people into your society who have absolutely nothing in common with you, then expect everything to be fine. Hopefully, we'll learn from their mistakes, and they'll be able to fix the problem before it's too late."

Tommy folded his arms. "Everything I'm seeing suggests it already is."

Leroux shrugged. "It may be. Brussels is supposed to be majority Muslim within fifteen years. Nothing you can do once that happens."

Tommy shuddered. "I don't know how you guys do this, day in and day out, knowing what's out there, and how blind so much of society is to it."

Leroux sighed, forcing a smile. "We live in a democracy. We have no control over what our leaders do beyond our individual vote, and we have no control over what the public does. All we can do is try to protect them from external threats, even if those threats are brought here willingly by the very people we're sworn to protect. I like to think that eventually we'll all figure out a way to get along, but you're right, it's easy to become jaded when you know what's really going on in the world, and realize how much of it is being whitewashed. It's a messed up time, and unfortunately, it's probably going to get much worse before it gets better."

"You think it will? Get better, I mean?"

Leroux nodded. "I do. We just need to keep doing our jobs so that we don't lose what we've worked so hard to build over the past centuries. We have to hope that people will eventually realize that we shouldn't change what we've built in order to accommodate those who come here with no intention of improving things." He held up a finger. "Sorry, I shouldn't have said that. It's not right."

"It might not be right, but it's the truth," said Tommy.

Sonya cleared her throat. "When my grandparents came here, they were given nothing. They arrived and immediately went to work. Life was hard for them, but their children were able to get an education. My dad became an engineer thanks to his parents, and my mom a doctor thanks to hers. They had me, and I grew up in a household that had its traditions from the homeland, but 99% of my life was as American as yours. We integrated, and now I don't even really think of myself as a hyphenated American. I'm just American, and I wouldn't have it any other way." She sighed. "I get frustrated with so many from my generation saying I have to identify with my heritage. I *have* to be an Asian-American, or a Chinese-American, or whatever. Why can't I just be American? I love my country, I've known no different, and I don't want to know any different. The moment you throw a hyphen in front of your identity, you've separated yourself from all the rest that don't share that same hyphenated qualifier. We keep tearing our country apart because we're this-American or that-American, instead of just American." She growled then sighed. "I'm sorry. As the only visible minority here, I just had to say something."

Tommy clapped and Leroux let him for a moment before holding up his hand and cutting him off. He smiled at Sonya. "I guess it's kind of liberating not being at the office and having to tiptoe around so many rules."

She flashed a smile, her eyes darting back to her clasped hands. "I guess. I'm sorry, I should have just kept my mouth shut."

Leroux shook his head. "No, you've got every right to express your opinion. We all do, as long as we recognize that not everyone is going to agree with that opinion, and that this is perfectly fine. Too often today, we see someone who disagrees with someone else say that person is an idiot, or more often than not, evil, and tries to have their opinion banned. It's ridiculous." He held up his hand as his heart rate climbed. "Okay, we really need to stop talking about this, otherwise I'm going to get myself worked up, and who knows what I'll say!"

Tommy was grinning. "I *love* this! Is this what a real job is like? I mean, I've only ever been at school. You can't say anything anymore unless you echo what the politically correct crowd tells you to say. If you do, you're shunned, attacked on social media, you can't find study partners, whatever. I always thought campus life was going to be so liberating, but college has been the most bullying, most restrictive environment I've ever been in. And I've been arrested!"

Leroux chuckled. "Yeah, I'm glad that's all behind me. I wouldn't want to be a student today who thought differently than what he's being told to think."

One of the machines beeped and Tommy turned his attention away from the off-topic conversation, smiling in triumph. "I've found our mystery woman from three weeks ago."

Sonya and Leroux rolled their chairs closer. "What have you got?"

Tommy brought up a video showing a woman entering the Minkin Holdings building. He tapped a few keys and the facial recognition points were matched then compared to the image they had of her from the poisoning in the UK, and from the bombing in Moscow.

"It's a match." Tommy turned toward them. "She was at all three locations. She's definitely our woman, and all these events are definitely connected."

Leroux bit down on his lip, staring at the images. "And we still have no idea who she is."

Sonya leaned forward, her elbows on her knees. "But this doesn't make sense. According to West, Minkin was in the room, giving the briefing. He was definitely involved. She's tried to kill the KGB agent who spotted the shooter, she's tried to kill the shooter, if Zorkin is correct, yet she didn't try to kill Minkin? Does that mean he's actually the one behind this?"

Leroux shook his head. "No, we're jumping to conclusions here. Just because she tried to get in the building doesn't mean she actually met with Minkin. She might have been there to kill him, and couldn't get to him."

"But what about the Novichok? We have to assume it came from him, and that he gave it to her. That's just too big a coincidence that one of the few civilians who would have access to it was also paid a visit by the woman who used the nerve agent."

Leroux agreed. "You're right, of course, it's too big a coincidence. But we don't know what happened there. There could have been a handoff by a third party, so she never had access to him, or she did meet with him, but the raid interfered with her plans, or, like you said, he's the one behind the whole thing, and she's just following his instructions."

Tommy sat listening to the conversation, his eyes wide, the smile genuine. He finally couldn't hold it in any longer. "Best! Job! Ever!"

Leroux laughed. "It is, isn't it? Now, let's hope Dylan can get some answers. We need to know what that woman was doing there, and more importantly, who the hell she is."

"And we need to find out where she is," said Sonya. "Before she hops a flight here and kills the Chief."

House on Mosfilmovskaya Apartments

Moscow, Russia

"Ms. Lobanov, my name is Dylan Kane. I'm from Shaw's of London. I'm here concerning your employer, Mr. Minkin. May I come up?"

He didn't blame the poor woman for hesitating. After all, Svetlana Lobanov's employer and boyfriend was in prison, awaiting trial for charges brought against him by a government drunk with power, a government that had shown no hesitation to kill those they felt opposed them. But he needed to speak with her, and his cover as an insurance investigator for Shaw's was his best hope.

"I, umm, don't know. I'm very tired. Perhaps later?"

"Ms. Lobanov, I'm here to help your employer. I need to speak to you. It is very urgent, otherwise we won't be able to assist him in these trying times, and I'm afraid he could go to prison for the rest of his life, or worse."

He heard a gasped cry, and wondered if she actually cared for Minkin, or just his wallet.

Perhaps a little of both.

"Very well. You can come up."

"Thank you, Ms. Lobanov." He handed the phone over to the woman manning the lobby desk, a few words exchanged before he was waved through.

"Fifteenth floor. Unit 1503."

Kane beamed a smile at the woman, her cheeks flushing slightly. He was looking good, a Tom Ford pinstripe suit tailored to his exact measurements was in the trunk of the car Zorkin had provided, along with all the accouterments needed to look drop-dead gorgeous. There was no better confidence builder than looking good, and no better panty remover than confidence.

And in the old days, he might have looked up the young lady when the job was done, but instead, the show he was putting on was all business, Fang the only woman he needed now.

I can't wait to get home.

It was an exciting feeling. For years, he rarely came home, for home wasn't really home. He spent so much time on assignment, and had been so damaged, that his downtime was spent at luxury resorts with bevies of women at his beck and call where he drowned out his sorrows and loneliness with alcohol and sex.

And when he did get a chance to go home to see his parents, he was met with a father who barely spoke to him because he was pissed Kane had given up his career in the military to be a "glorified insurance salesman," and a family he had to lie to about everything he did.

But it was different now. When the Assembly had kidnapped his parents to get to him, they had finally become aware of what he was doing for a living, and the relationship between him and them, especially his father, was stronger than ever. And with Fang in his life, he had a home to come back to.

My old stomping grounds probably think I'm dead.

He stepped onto the elevator and pressed the button for the fifteenth floor, arriving moments later. He checked himself in the mirrored wall then stepped off, heading for 1503. He knocked and the door was opened, a stunning blond woman greeting him with red eyes and flushed cheeks.

Man or money? Money or man?

"Ms. Lobanov, I'm Dylan Kane. May I come in?"

"Of course." She stepped aside and he entered, taking in the opulent apartment, no expense spared to keep her happy.

Secretaries make good money in Russia.

The door closed behind him and she headed for a nearby wet bar, refilling a martini glass. She held it up. "Do you want one?"

He waved it off. "No, thank you." He motioned toward a sitting area. "Please, let's talk for a few minutes, then I'll let you get on with your day."

She stumbled over her own feet and he rushed forward, grabbing her arm and preventing a faceplant. "Th-thank you." She sighed and allowed herself to be led to a nearby chair. "I'm afraid you've caught me at my worst."

Kane smiled, taking a seat beside her, turning his chair to face her. He leaned in, gently squeezing her arm. "You have nothing to apologize for. These are stressful times."

"You have no idea."

Kane pulled a folder from his briefcase, flipping it open then pulling a pen from his shirt pocket. "I'll try to be brief." He pretended to scan his notes. "Now, your name is Svetlana Lobanov?"

"Yes."

"And you are Mr. Minkin's secretary."

"Executive Assistant."

"Of course, forgive me. So, that means you manage all of his appointments?"

"Yes."

"And when the police raided the offices, were you there?"

"Yes."

"And was Mr. Minkin meeting with someone?"

She hesitated. "Umm, why?"

"I need as much information as possible if we're going to mount an effective defense."

Her eyes widened. "You're a lawyer?"

He shook his head. "No, but the firm I represent has plenty of lawyers. Right now, we need to determine if Mr. Minkin is at fault for his arrest. If he is innocent, his policy will provide him with the best defense money can buy. But I need to know the absolute truth. What we're getting from the government, frankly, isn't helpful."

"He's innocent! I swear it!"

Kane smiled, patting her arm again. "I'm sure he is, and I'm sure you want to help him. And the best way you can do that is to tell me everything you know." He stared back at his notes for show. "Now, was Mr. Minkin meeting with someone when the police raid occurred?"

Again, she hesitated, though only for a moment. "Yes."

"And the name of that person?"

She shook her head. "I don't know."

Kane regarded her. "You don't know, or you can't remember?"

"I don't know. He made the appointment himself and only told me to block off the time. I don't know who she was."

"She?"

"Yes."

Kane removed a photo of their suspect and held it up. "Is this—"

"That's her! She tried to kill Yury!"

Kane's eyebrows shot up. "Excuse me?"

"When the police raid began, I entered his office to tell him, and she was attacking him with a letter opener."

"A letter opener?"

"Yes."

"Then what happened?"

"Yury told me to lock the doors and go for lunch, and to not come back until I heard from him."

"What about the woman? What happened to her?"

She shrugged. "I don't know, but I never got a chance to leave. The police were already on the floor. When they went in Yury's office, they brought him out, but not the woman."

Kane leaned back in his chair. "Interesting. Where do you think she went?"

"She had to have gone down Yury's private elevator. That's the only possibility."

"And where does it lead?"

"Well, any floor he wants, but only he has access, so he must have put her in. She must have gone to the basement level. There's an escape route that almost nobody knows about."

"But you know."

She blushed. "Yury used it to get me in and out when his, umm, well."

Kane chuckled. "It's okay, Ms. Lobanov, my firm represented your husband during the, shall we say, scandal. I know everything."

She sighed, her shoulders slumping. "That's a relief. I hate lying, but I love Yury so much." She eyed him. "Do you believe in destiny, Mr. Kane?"

Kane regarded her for a moment. If he had been asked that a few years ago, he would have said no, but the number of things that had to have gone wrong in the world, and the number of things that had to go right to bring him and Fang together, made him a believer. "Yes."

She smiled broadly. "Then you're a romantic like me!"

"I suppose I am. And two people meant to be together should never be kept apart."

"Exactly!" She leaned forward and patted his knee. "You *do* understand!"

Kane brought them back on track, the woman now putty in his hands, two hopeless romantics working together to thwart the powers trying to prevent destiny. "Now, why wouldn't he have gone with her?"

"Would you get on an elevator with a woman who just tried to kill you?"

Kane laughed. "I suppose not. But if she had just tried to do that, why do you think he saved her?"

Her eyes darted away and she became uncomfortable. "I, umm, don't know."

Kane leaned forward, lowering his voice. "I think you do, and I think the Russian government knows too. The only way we can prepare for his defense is if we know everything."

She sighed. "Very well." She stared him in the eyes, the earnestness making the cynic in him wonder if she truly did, in fact, love Minkin. "I can't be sure, mind you, but I think he was giving her something. Something, umm, well, not good."

"Not good?"

"Somebody arrived with a briefcase just before the meeting. They met for only a few seconds, then the man left, without the briefcase. He seemed very nervous when he entered, but almost relieved when he left. I think he was scared of what was in that briefcase, so I guess that means it was something bad."

"And the woman, when did she show up?"

"Only minutes later."

"And you think he gave her this briefcase?"

She shook her head. "No, but I think he gave her what was inside it."

Kane's eyes narrowed. "I don't understand. What makes you think that?"

"Because I was there, remember? The police were holding me in the hallway, so I saw everything. They led poor Yury out in handcuffs. I told them that he was innocent, that some woman had just tried to kill him and that they should be arresting her, then I watched as some men in those special suits, oooh, what are they called?"

"Hazmat suits?"

Her eyes widened and she bounced in her chair, the twins putting on a show. "Yes, that's it! They went inside, and a few minutes later came out with the briefcase wrapped in some clear plastic bags."

"And you're sure it was the same briefcase?"

"Yes. It was metal, silver or something. Yury would never carry something so tacky."

"Did they question you about the woman?"

"Yes. I gave them a description, told them what I saw, then that was it. We were all sent home."

"Have you been questioned since?"

She shook her head. "No. Which kind of surprises me."

Kane frowned. "Me too." Though if this was all about the stolen Novichok, then perhaps he shouldn't be surprised. The conversation had confirmed a few things he was already fairly certain about, yet left the most critical questions still unanswered. They now knew the same suspect was likely handed the nerve agent personally by Minkin. She had then tried to kill Minkin, which made sense, since she was trying to kill people involved in the plot, and they knew from West that Minkin was in the room giving the briefing. Minkin had obviously had her whisked away in his private elevator so he wouldn't be put in the same room with the nerve agent as the police stormed his offices, which was why she wasn't caught. The secretary—executive assistant—had told the police about her, they had obviously issued a bulletin to have her picked up, then it was canceled by someone.

Yet who that someone was, who the woman was, and who was supplying her with information she couldn't possibly know, were all critical questions, and all questions that remained unanswered.

Minkin had to know as least some of those answers, which meant he had to meet the man.

He looked at Svetlana. "I need to meet with Mr. Minkin."

"Yes, do that! You'll see he's innocent."

He smiled. "I believe you, I really do. But unfortunately, the authorities won't let me. I've already tried."

She closed her eyes, her shoulders rolling inward as she folded her arms. "Then what are we going to do?" Her jaw dropped and her eyes widened. "I could ask him your questions!"

Kane's eyebrows shot up. "You're seeing him?"

She blushed. "Yes, in a few hours. In fact, I have to start getting ready. It's an, umm, what do they call it? A visit for a man and a woman?"

"Conjugal?"

She blushed some more. "Exactly."

It must be nice to have money.

"Then you better start getting ready. You don't want to disappoint destiny."

She beamed a smile at him. "What do you want me to ask him?"

"Only two things. What was the name of the woman, and who arranged the meeting?"

Her eyes narrowed. "Wouldn't she have?"

"Perhaps, but I have a feeling she didn't."

"Why?"

"Just a suspicion. If you could ask him those two questions for me, then I'll see you later tonight and you can tell me, okay?"

She smiled, reaching out her hand and grasping his. "We're going to save him, aren't we?"

He returned the smile. "With your help, absolutely."

Outside Pechatniki Pre-trial Detention Center

Moscow, Russia

Boykov tapped Moriz Grekov on the shoulder, startling the old guard. The man smiled, few words having been exchanged after the arranged meeting between "brothers."

"So, did it go well?"

Boykov grinned. "*Very* well. So well, in fact, that we must talk privately, now."

Grekov scratched his chin. "I was going to grab a drink if you want to join me."

Boykov shook his head. "No, nobody can hear what I have to say. It's about my brother's generosity, if you know what I mean."

Grekov's face lit up. "My place?"

"No, my hotel is very close. Let's head over there. I've got a few bottles of vodka on ice waiting for us."

The smile broadened, and they were soon into the first bottle in one of the nastier hotel rooms in the city. Grekov drained his shot and slammed the glass onto the table.

"So, tell me, did you and your brother reconcile?"

Boykov nodded, finishing his own drink. "We did. He was far more understanding than I had expected, and we were able to say our goodbyes. I do hope to see him again soon, though I know I can't expect you to be sneaking me in again."

"Perhaps if you come to visit him formally, he'll let you."

Boykov shook his head. "No, he expressly forbade it. He's concerned that if the authorities find out he has a long lost brother, they'll use me to get to him."

Grekov frowned, pouring them two more. "That's a good point. I hadn't thought of that. I wouldn't put anything past those bastards."

"Me neither." Boykov took a sip of his drink. "Which is why I'm going to ask you for one final favor."

Grekov paused. "Umm, I don't know."

Boykov's eyes shot wide for show. "Oh, I almost forgot in all the excitement!" He grabbed a laptop off the bed and flipped it open, tapping a few keys. "I told you my brother was a generous man." He flipped the screen around so Grekov could see the balance on the account set up earlier that day for the soon to be retired guard.

Grekov dropped his glass, thankfully only on the tabletop. "What, umm, what am I looking at?"

"Half a million Euros, in an account in Geneva under your name." He slipped an envelope across the table containing the account information and a bank card, Minkin's people true to their word and efficient.

Grekov's cheeks paled and he gripped the arms of the chair as he struggled to not faint. "Are-are you serious?"

Boykov grinned. "Yup. It's all yours. Half a million Euros." He tapped the envelope. "Everything you need to access it is in there." He leaned forward. "And I can double that if you want."

Grekov tore his eyes away from the screen. "Double?"

"Yes. All I need to know is when my brother is being taken to the courthouse. I know it's a little risky, but I'll just sit in the back of the court so I can see him again." He sighed. "I haven't been feeling well today. I think I've been running on hope, just trying to see my brother and patch things up with him, and now that I have, my body knows it's time to let go. To give up."

Grekov frowned. "You shouldn't think like that. Surely your brother can help? Get you the best doctors?"

Boykov shook his head. "No, my time is up, but I would love to see my brother just one more time, to be there to support him, you know? If he just saw me in the courthouse, he'd know I meant everything I said today."

Grekov's head bobbed slowly, his eyes drifting back to the balance on the laptop. "Double?"

"Double. I just need to know what time he's leaving for the courthouse so I have enough time to get there before him."

Grekov sucked in a deep breath then nodded. "They briefed us just before I left. Ten tomorrow morning."

Pechatniki Pre-trial Detention Center

Moscow, Russia

Minkin smiled as Svetlana stepped into the room, but did nothing as the guard who had shown her in let his eyes roam her incredible body for a few seconds before finally closing the door.

And she burst into tears the moment the lock clicked.

"Oh, darling, what a horrible place! I can't stand that you're in here!"

He wrapped his arms around her, the little blue pill already doing its job as he was determined to get every moment of pleasure he could out of her two-hour visit.

And he had no time to waste on tears.

He was well over twice her age, and though he did care for her, perhaps even deeply, she could be replaced at the drop of a hat, though not so easily from within the confines of these walls. But if Boykov came through, then his days behind bars might be numbered, and once freed, he'd disappear and live off the massive sums he had stashed around the world.

The Russian government would never find him, nor would that insane bitch who had tried to kill him.

But her uncle?

Cheslav Aristov was rich, though nowhere near as rich as he was. He was well-connected, and a member of the Duma. He had never met the man, and only knew him through reputation. He was someone you didn't want to disappoint, which was the only reason why he had agreed to steal the Novichok and deliver it to his niece.

It had been an idiotic move. Though no one had said anything yet, he knew that was why he had been arrested. From what his lawyers had gathered, the theft had been detected immediately, and they had tracked the courier to see where he was delivering it.

Straight into the Minkin Holdings building.

The raid had been quickly coordinated, executed, and thanks to his quick thinking in sending the woman down his private elevator, they were going apeshit trying to find it before it was too late.

And it was too late.

Apparently, she had used it on her target in London, the news reports now suggesting the target was former KGB. Minkin didn't recognize the photos, yet he must have somehow been involved in the assassination plot, since the woman had said that's who she wanted to kill. Yet he had been in the room, and was certain that man wasn't, though he couldn't be sure. There were no names used that day during the briefing, and faces changed a lot over thirty years, though surely he'd recognize the man. He had recognized Boykov, after all.

Then again, he barely recognized himself in the mirror anymore, his wrinkled, weathered face no longer what it once was in 1988.

"I have good news."

He began undressing Svetlana between the tears and sniffles, his need about to become painful if it wasn't satisfied. "What's that?"

"A man from your insurance company came to see me today."

He paused. "My insurance company?"

"I think that's what he said. I'm sorry, I had a little bit to drink. I've been so depressed."

He resumed unbuttoning her outfit. "What did he want?"

"He was asking me questions about the day you were arrested."

He paused again. "And you answered them?"

"Of course! He said he needed to know what happened so they could prepare your defense."

"I thought you said he was from an insurance company." He mauled her breasts, finally freed, her response muffled.

"He said they'd be supplying the lawyers if they thought you were innocent."

He came up for air. "Of course I'm innocent. You told him that, right?"

She moaned. "Of course." She grabbed him by both sides of his head, pushing him away as she stared down at him. "But you have to answer two questions he had. I promised him."

He pushed her onto the bed and began removing her shoes as she hiked her skirt down. "What questions?"

"What was the name of the woman you were meeting with?"

He paused. It was a reasonable question, though why his insurance company was asking questions a lawyer should be, he wasn't sure. He forced himself to stop.

Insurance company?

He wasn't thinking straight. He was so horny, so preoccupied, that he was barely listening to what she was saying. He reached down and tore her pantyhose open where it counted. "I have to have you. Now!" He dropped his pants and underwear in one swift move, Little Minkin waving hello.

"What was her name?"

"I don't know." He climbed onto the bed, positioning himself.

"You don't know?"

"No, I was never told her name, and she never said it. I didn't want to know."

"Then how did you meet her? I mean, who set up the meeting?"

He groaned as he finally got what he wanted. "Her uncle set it up."

She grabbed onto him, pulling him closer. "What's his name?"

"I don't give a shit right now!"

"I need to know. I have to tell him the name."

He couldn't stop himself if he wanted to, but whoever this asshole insurance guy was, he was ruining what should be a fantastic time with the best lay he had ever had. He growled as he flipped onto his back, letting her do the work.

"What's. His. Name?"

"It's too dangerous." He moaned. "I can't tell you."

"Please, darling, I want to help!" She cried out, and he couldn't care less if she were faking.

"I'll tell him myself when I get out of here."

He cursed.

I shouldn't have said that. This moron is liable to tell everyone.

She stopped, staring down at him with a big smile. "You're getting out?"

He shoved up with his hips, urging her to continue. "I mean, when I win my court case."

She resumed, and he sighed with relief. "Oh, it sounded like it might be soon."

"Hopefully." She opened her mouth to ask yet another distracting question and he reached up, clamping a hand over her mouth. "No more questions. Just sex."

She nodded, her reply muffled, and he didn't care.

He just wanted to forget his troubles for now, and worry later about who the hell this insurance company rep was, and why he was asking questions he shouldn't be.

Yet as he continued writhing underneath the spectacular beauty that was Svetlana, he couldn't help but wonder who the man was. His questions suggested he was trying to find out who he had given the Novichok to, so he couldn't have been sent by the woman or by her uncle, Cheslav Aristov. And if the woman was targeting those involved in the assassination plot in 1988, then this man couldn't be involved in that either, otherwise he wouldn't ask who she was.

He growled in frustration.

She stopped. "What is it?"

"It's this man. He's distracting me. Are you seeing him again?"

"Yes, tonight. I'm supposed to give him the answers to his questions."

"Tell him I'll meet with him as soon as I'm out of here."

"But he needs the answers to help you in court. If he doesn't have them, then he can't help you, so you might be found guilty."

He frowned.

She's smarter than she looks.

"I'll let you in on a little secret, so long as you promise to not say another word the entire time you're here."

She nodded.

"I'll be out of here before I set foot in any courtroom." He grabbed her hips. "Now get back to work."

House on Mosfilmovskaya Apartments

Moscow, Russia

Svetlana unlocked the door to her apartment and stepped inside, swiping her hand on the panel to the right of the door, activating the lights. She was happy, her troubles forgotten for the moment, memories of the two hours spent together with Yury bringing constant smiles to her face.

Except when he treated her like garbage.

What was it with men that they thought they could talk so horribly to their partners, especially during sex? He was much older than her, from a generation where women weren't treated with as much respect. And the fact he was Russian didn't help. She had dated some Westerners. Two Americans and a Brit. They treated her better than she had ever been treated, but those were always short-term relationships while they were on business in Moscow. They'd never take her back with them, and she didn't want them to.

She loved Russia. It had its problems, but when you were rich, those problems were easily forgotten. And if you were pretty, and open-minded, finding someone rich to take care of you was easy enough.

Enter Yury Minkin.

They had met through friends, and had hit it off immediately. Her plying him with alcohol, and his failing marriage certainly helped. She had gone back to his hotel room the very first night, and by the end of it, she knew he was hers. This apartment was given to her, plus a generous allowance, and her sugar daddy had access to her whenever he wanted.

And once the press was silenced—through death threats, she assumed—he had hired her to be his executive assistant, a job she wasn't very good at, but it gave him access to her whenever he needed some relief, relief she was happy to provide so long as he kept the troubled world that surrounded them at a distance.

Maybe you don't love Russia as much as you think.

She tossed her jacket on the back of a chair and kicked her heels off. She headed for the shower, peeling her clothes off as she went, tossing them on the floor, leaving a trail of depravity for the maid to pick up the next morning. She turned on the shower, and was about to step inside, when the doorbell rang.

She cursed.

It had to be the insurance agent, or representative, or whatever he had called himself. She had left instructions at the front desk that he should be sent up immediately, and was now regretting it. She stared at herself in the mirror for a moment, debating on whether she should greet him naked. He was cute. Very cute. And she was horny. Sex with Yury was never very satisfying, though he did try. And she was happy to make him happy, though that didn't satisfy the needs she had.

An insurance agent my age might be nice.

She frowned.

But what if it isn't him?

She grabbed a towel and wrapped it around herself, making certain the girls were on display, then headed for the door as it rang a second time. She opened and beamed a smile at the startled agent.

"I was hoping it was you."

He smiled, extending a hand. She let go of the towel and shook it, the Egyptian cotton creation falling to the floor, revealing all.

His smile broadened, and he didn't look away. "Let me help you with that." He knelt, picked up the towel, then handed it to her.

She took it, but didn't put it on. "Thank you."

"May I come in?"

She stared at him coyly. "You can do whatever you want."

He stepped inside and closed the door as she tossed the towel over her shoulder, strutting over to the wet bar. "Martini?"

"Absolutely."

Shivers ran across her body from the chill in the apartment, and the anticipation of what might be. She prepared the drinks and noted that this time, rather than sitting in a chair, he had sat on the couch, his arm spread across the back. She bent over, giving him a show, and handed him his drink before sitting beside him, curling her legs up and turning to face him.

"I, umm, have to admit, I wasn't expecting a greeting like this."

She ran a finger down his chest as she took a sip. "Does it make you uncomfortable?"

His head shook a little too quickly. "No, umm, not at all."

What a sweetie!

He took a long drink. "So, did you see Mr. Minkin?"

"Let's talk about that later." She nodded toward the bedroom. "I have a shower running. Do you want to join me?"

He gulped. "Umm, sure, but, umm, how about we get our business out of the way first?"

She smiled. "Then I have you all night?"

He flushed. "As long as you want me."

She snuggled closer, leaning in, a hair's breadth separating their lips. "I might never let you go."

"That sounds like something I could go for." His voice was hoarse, desperate. He wanted her, and he wanted her bad, and there was no doubt the feeling was mutual, her entire body tingling with what wonders lay behind this impeccably dressed man. He cleared his throat, pulling away, though only a few inches. “So, your meeting. Did it happen?”

She frowned, her shoulders slumping as the mood was broken with thoughts of her aging sugar daddy. “Yes.”

“And did you ask him the questions?”

“I did.”

“And?”

“Take off your shirt and I’ll tell you.”

“Hey, we agreed, business first.”

She pouted. “I just want to make sure I’m getting something worthwhile in trade.”

He sighed and stood, removing his suit jacket. She grabbed him by the tie and pulled him closer, removing it as he unbuttoned his shirt, revealing pecs and abs to die for.

A body she had to have.

She grabbed his belt, yanking her prize closer.

“Wait, business first.”

She frowned. “Fine. He didn’t know her name. The meeting was arranged by her uncle. He knows his name but wouldn’t give it to me because it’s too dangerous. He wants to meet with you to discuss it. There, business done.” She grabbed him by the crotch. “Now let’s get down to business.”

“When will he meet me?”

“Soon.”

"At the prison?"

She shook her head as she concentrated on his zipper. "No, I don't think so. He seemed to think he'd be getting out very soon."

He grabbed her hand as she reached inside his pants. "What do you mean?"

She growled in frustration and stared up at him. "He said he'd never see the inside of a courtroom." She yanked her hand away and grabbed his ass, pulling him closer. "So, are we done talking?"

He nodded. "Yes." Then he stepped back. "I'm afraid I have to report back to my office. Can I take a raincheck on this?"

She stared up at him, dumbfounded. "Are you kidding me?"

Off-the-books Operations Center

Outside Bethesda, Maryland

"I found her!"

Leroux snapped awake in his chair, wiping away a bit of drool with the back of his hand. Sonya was already scooting toward Tommy's workstation, and nobody seemed to have noticed his body's embarrassing betrayal. "What was that?"

Sonya glanced at him. "I should have woken you to tell you to go to bed, but you, umm, looked so peaceful." She blushed then pointed at the screen. "Tommy's found her!"

He yawned. "Who?"

Tommy grinned. "Our blonde. Her name is Natasha Ivashin. I'm running her name now, but it's definitely her."

Leroux scooted closer. "Where did you find her?"

"In some old photos from an MMA group in Moscow. They have thousands of photos on their Facebook page, and she's in quite a few of them by the looks of it." He tapped his keyboard, bringing up several photos his program had matched with their suspect's facial recognition points. "As you can see, she was an MMA fighter a few years ago. These photos I'm finding her in all date back five to ten years." A photo appeared showing a rather muscular looking woman. "Jeez, looks like she could have been on the East German Women's Wrestling team."

Leroux chuckled. "Good reference."

"Top Secret. Awesome movie. Still holds up."

"I forgot all about that one. I saw it as a kid. Val Kilmer in his prime." Leroux made a mental note to watch it again soon. "Okay, hit every database we can. We need to find out everything about her. I want to know where she lives, where she lived, who she works for, her complete résumé. I want to know about relatives, especially her father. Who's alive, who's dead. Everything."

"Got it."

Sonya turned to him. "What databases can we tap?"

"Tap them all, including CIA. I spoke to the Chief, and now that we know our side's involvement was limited to Agent West, he feels confident we can trust our people. He still wants to minimize exposure, though."

"Can we move to a proper location?" asked Sonya, hope in her eyes.

Leroux nodded. "We can, but if we do, we lose Tommy because he doesn't have clearance."

Tommy appeared crestfallen at the notion, and Sonya noticed.

She smiled. "Well, I guess we can keep going here." Then yawned. "Can we bring in somebody, though?"

Leroux chuckled. "Nope. Nobody can know about this place, remember? And like I said, the Chief wants to minimize exposure."

She cursed. "Oh well. Being wedged in here is good training for the upcoming apocalypse."

Leroux smiled. "That's the spirit!"

House on Mosfilmovskaya Apartments

Moscow, Russia

Kane fixed his tie in the elevator's mirror as he calmed his libido. Svetlana was a gorgeous woman, and if it were operationally necessary, he would have thrown himself into the role, but it wasn't. He had what he needed from her, perhaps more than the poor girl realized.

Minkin was planning on breaking out of jail.

The elevator chimed and he gasped as he noticed his fly was still undone, Mr. Happy poking out for a look. He adjusted himself and zipped his fly as the doors opened. He positioned his briefcase strategically to hide the fact he was still a red-blooded male despite being in a committed relationship, and headed for the door, nodding his goodnight to the woman manning the front desk.

Outside, the brisk Moscow winter made its presence felt, and he hurried to the car provided by Zorkin, climbing inside and firing up the engine. He turned on anything that could provide heat, then checked the secure app on his phone for messages.

We have her name. Natasha Ivashin.

He smiled at the message from Leroux. It was only a matter of time before he found her, but if Leroux's team could discover her identity, then so could the authorities. It was a race to get to her first. He feared that she was merely a replaceable pawn. He needed to know who she was working for, and why, after thirty years, they were trying to clean up after themselves, otherwise Morrison could remain in danger.

And Russians too often shot first then didn't ask the questions they feared the answers to.

He was no longer convinced the Russian government was involved, though the Western press and off the record government officials were certain it was state sanctioned. The Novichok was the key, but nobody beyond probably the Russian government knew Minkin was responsible for that, and they were keeping that tidbit to themselves, likely waiting for the right moment to release it and embarrass the American and British governments.

He was certain Minkin had stolen the Novichok nerve agent, provided it to this Natasha Ivashin, who then used it to poison Kulick. How she knew to do that was the question. Very few people could have known Kulick's involvement as a witness to the assassination attempt. He wasn't involved beyond spotting the sniper, yet she had known to target him.

And why target him?

It had to be either a revenge plot, or a complete containment situation. This wasn't a mission to punish those who had tried to kill Gorbachev, otherwise Kulick would never have been a target. A containment situation would include anyone who knew, including Kulick and Morrison, despite their innocence. A revenge plot would only target those the person blamed.

He paused, the first hints of heat emerging from the vents.

It would only target those they blamed.

Blamed for what? By targeting Kulick, if it were a revenge plot, then they obviously blamed him for something.

Preventing the assassination by recognizing Boykov?

That made sense, and if it were the case, then Morrison would be on their radar if they knew who he was.

And she had targeted Boykov, the shooter. Why? Was it because he failed in his mission? That was possible.

And those possibilities narrowed the suspect pool. If it were a revenge plot, it had to be someone involved. The guard involved that Morrison had found dead was killed by Boykov. If it were someone related to the dead Russian, then they wouldn't blame Kulick or Morrison. They would only blame Boykov and those who ordered him to kill the man.

And then there was Minkin, the man who had given the briefing, but who this Natasha had tried to kill moments before the police raid, a raid whose timing was far too coincidental to not be related to the Novichok. That ruled him and his relations out as well.

Everything came back to the two men whose identities they had no clue of.

Could one of them be her uncle?

If he arranged the meeting with Minkin, then it made sense he also told her that Minkin was involved. She tried to kill him with a letter opener. It was doable, but a trained assassin would have succeeded where she failed.

He leaned his head back against the seat.

She's not a pro.

Would a pro have allowed themselves to be caught on camera in London, planting the nerve agent? Yes, because the UK was drowning with surveillance cameras, but would they have made it so obvious? Would they have timed it so poorly that their victim opened the gate for them?

She was working alone.

Pros would have at least been working in pairs. A lookout would have given her the signal that the targets were approaching, giving her plenty of time to plant the nerve agent and leave without risking an encounter. And pros would have planted it far earlier in a far more innocent manner. In this case, the CCTV footage made it so obvious she was responsible, there was no doubt.

No, she was acting on her own.

Yet she wasn't. Her uncle had arranged the meeting, according to Svetlana. And more importantly, Minkin had actually handed over the Novichok.

Why would he do that?

He was rich. Extremely rich. Leroux's file on the man indicated he was worth billions. There was no amount of money that could be offered to a man like that, that would make him handover a deadly nerve agent, that once found out, would leave him facing life in prison or worse.

No, the only reason Minkin would hand over the nerve agent would be if he was afraid for his life.

He's scared of the uncle.

Who was this uncle? Was he involved? Was he one of the two men they didn't have identities for?

That made sense, but if he was, why would he use his own niece to clean up his own past?

That didn't make sense.

The man had to be powerful, someone to be feared, otherwise there was no way Minkin would have done what he had done.

Could she be the one out for revenge?

He chewed his cheek as his mind raced. If this were a revenge plot, which he was now more inclined to believe, then perhaps she was related to someone who had died as a result of the failed plot. The KGB were the types to clean up their failures, so if a participant were executed, and she was to discover the truth all these years later, then it might make sense that she seek revenge. She could go to her rich, powerful uncle, ask him for help, and he agrees, using his money and contacts to assist her along the way.

But why?

Love?

He doubted that.

A smile spread.

For revenge as well!

It's her *uncle*. If her father was the one for whom she was seeking revenge, then it was quite possible they were brothers, and he too would want payback. He'd be of the right age to have possibly been in the Soviet military, or even the KGB, so could have contacts from the old days, and if KGB, the ruthlessness to want to seek blood.

Yet why wouldn't he have done so before? If he had the means to threaten a man like Minkin into stealing a deadly nerve agent, then he had it last year, he had it ten years ago.

Though perhaps not. Money came and went, as did power. Perhaps everything had come together perfectly at this point in time.

He shook his head.

You wouldn't use your own niece.

When the timing was right, he would take action. No, this was *her* revenge plot, a plot that her uncle was helping her with, and might even endorse if it was his brother, but it was something he must not have known about before.

She discovered the truth, and brought it to him.

Maybe he wasn't aware of what had happened to his brother, and once revealed, he too wanted to take action. But why was everything so elaborate? Novichok? Bombing an apartment building? Bullets to the head were much simpler.

Misdirection?

The Russian government was being blamed for the nerve agent attack, regardless of who delivered the poison. Islamic extremists were initially blamed for the bombing, though that was now being questioned, many still blaming them, claiming she was a convert or a black widow in disguise.

Was it all designed to give her time to complete the task?

Yet the methods used made things far more complex than they needed to be.

It's a message.

Now *that* made sense. A message was being sent to the others, though to warn them she was coming didn't make sense. Then again, would those involved thirty years ago know each other now? Kulick was a lowly KGB agent at the time, and off everyone's radar since. Boykov, who had apparently survived the detonation, would have been one of dozens on a list of victims, his name an alias that few, if any, would have noticed, and any message that might have been intended would have been missed.

He sighed.

None of it made sense, but they were getting closer. The uncle was the key.

Find him, we find her. And hopefully everyone else involved.

Pechatniki Pre-trial Detention Center

Moscow, Russia

Moriz Grekov's heart hammered. What he had done had gone against everything he believed in as a guard. He had served honorably for almost twenty years, this the best, most secure job he had ever found, and now he had betrayed his comrades over money.

He was an idiot.

He should have known something else was going on. A man buys him a drink, and by coincidence his brother is a prisoner in a jail that he's a guard at? It was laughable now that he thought of it in the sober light of day.

Though nothing had happened by arranging the visit, the possibility of piles of rubles floating in front of his eyelids every time he closed them, telling his hungover mind to just ignore the obvious fact he was being used. After all, he had to be at least seventy, so what could he possibly do? Grekov had watched the man like a hawk on the security monitors, and nothing untoward had happened. The visit had been brief, Minkin had said nothing to him when it was done, and the man had been shown out.

They had gotten away with it, and it was over.

But when the money had been shown to him, all judgment was tossed, the time of the court transfer blurted out before he could think straight, the greed, the possibility of a secure retirement for his children, had forced him to be stupid.

For this had to be a prison break.

It had to be. Minkin's "brother" knew the transfer time, and had wanted to know it in advance. If he genuinely wanted to be at the courtroom to be with his brother, he could have simply asked for a text message once the transfer was complete. And that wasn't the only hole in the story. The courtroom was closed. There would be no audience. Everyone knew that. In fact, he was quite certain he had said that to him in their initial encounter at the bar, though they were both drunk, and it was plausible the man forgot.

But he wasn't his brother. He couldn't be.

Yet Minkin had said nothing.

They're working together.

It was the only explanation. The man had used him to get inside, met with Minkin, then exchanged what information was needed to plan the escape. If that weren't the case, then Minkin would have said something.

And a million Euros?

That was money meant to buy his silence, not thank him for reuniting two brothers.

The man's worth billions. Maybe a million is nothing to him.

It was possible. He growled to himself as Minkin appeared, hands and feet cuffed, the chains linking them causing him to shuffle out the back entrance where a heavy guard was present.

Including himself.

Normally, he didn't accompany prisoners on these types of transfers, but he had been added to the team, as were many others, the powers that be obviously concerned about an attempt to free one of the wealthiest men in Russia, a man who had many contacts in the military realm.

And Grekov's assignment to the team was what had his heart pounding, sweat drenching his shirt under his bullet-resistant vest, his glasses steaming from his perspiring forehead.

We're all going to die.

He wanted to warn them, to tell them what was about to happen, yet he couldn't be positive he was right. What if the story was true? What if they *were* brothers? What if this billionaire tossed him the equivalent of a few coins as thanks? What if they truly did want to see each other in court one last time?

If there was a chance, no matter how remote, that the story could be true, and he told his superiors what he had done, he'd be tossed in prison for the rest of his life, a life that wouldn't be very long, as police never survived past the first few months.

And even if the story were complete bullshit as he suspected, and they were about to be attacked, he might still survive, and nobody would know he was involved if he kept his mouth shut.

He sighed as he followed his comrades in arms out the rear entrance and into the bright morning sunlight, the frosty weather causing the sweat that drenched his body to instantly send a harsh chill throughout.

He was committed now.

He just prayed that he survived, along with the others.

Or that the man who had changed his future, for the better or worse, was telling the truth.

Minkin climbed into the back of the prison transport, an armored affair nearly impossible to open for the average escapee, though he was anything but average. With his billions, and his contacts, he had little doubt he was about to be a free man. His KGB career had prepared him well for life after the collapse. Not only had he leveraged the information he had on the new leadership into lucrative chunks of state assets during the privatization boom after the collapse of socialism, he had cultivated contacts on the "other" side of the law to do his bidding whenever it became necessary.

And those contacts would do anything he asked.

As was proven when he had given the orders to steal the Novichok nerve agent.

It had been done, without hesitation, and they were successful.

To a point.

Unfortunately, the asset had been caught in the act and followed. It was the only explanation for the sequence of events.

And his jailors knew this, which was why he and his lawyers had been kept in the dark on all court dates.

He spotted the guard he had paid off and suppressed a smile, making certain to avoid eye contact. The fact the transfer was still taking place as scheduled, meant the man had kept his mouth shut, despite being assigned to the detail that might very well be wiped out in the next few minutes.

He didn't want any of them to die. He wasn't a monster, yet he also didn't want to spend the rest of his life in a Russian prison. Yes, he had supplied the Novichok, but he had no choice. One doesn't go against a member of the Russian parliament, especially a man like Aristov, whom he knew by reputation to be ruthless in business and life, including his past Soviet life.

One didn't ignore "requests" by men like that.

Otherwise you die, or worse.

Fortunately, the nerve agent had only harmed two people, who according to the press reports, might survive. The incidental poisonings were minor, so in the end, his actions really didn't have serious consequences beyond embarrassing the Russian state.

And that was why he had to escape, for he had little doubt any trial would lead to a guaranteed guilty verdict, and any prison stay enforced brutality, his money buying him little extra should the glorious leader dictate it.

His life of luxury and comfort was over the moment the gavel dropped.

Unless today went perfectly.

He sat, his chains locked to a loop on the floor, the convoy underway moments later.

He closed his eyes and widened his stance, preparing for whatever it was that was to come.

Off-the-books Operations Center

Outside Bethesda, Maryland

"The convoy is underway."

Leroux stood behind Sonya and Tommy, all of them merely observing, no action to be taken on their part. Kane was convinced an escape attempt was imminent, and that was a Russian problem. Given the state of relations between the former Soviet Union and most of the rest of the world, Morrison had decided no warning would be given.

They wanted Minkin freed.

It was the only way they were going to question him, to find out what was going on. The woman, so far, was leading to a near dead end. Natasha Ivashin was a nobody. A math teacher at a local high school, with no government connections. Her mother had recently died, and her father had committed suicide almost thirty years ago.

The timing of his suicide suggested he might have been involved in the assassination plot, yet there was one critical problem.

Natasha Ivashin had no uncles. Her parents had no surviving relatives, and any siblings had been sisters.

There were no uncles to be found in her family tree.

That meant either Minkin had lied to Svetlana, which was a definite possibility, or he had been lied to himself.

Though there was one thing Kane seemed certain of, and Leroux was inclined to agree with. Minkin knew who arranged the meeting, otherwise he would never have stolen the Novichok.

They had to put Minkin and Kane together, which meant they had to track Minkin over the next thirty minutes, no matter what. Losing him would likely mean losing him forever.

"They've cleared the jail perimeter," said Sonya as they all watched the feed from a tiny drone Kane had deployed, its controls now tagged to track the vehicle they had watched Minkin get loaded into.

"It's just a matter of time." Leroux patted the back of Sonya's chair. "If this goes down, make sure that drone's tracking is switched to the correct vehicle. If it's not, we may never pick him up again."

Sonya nodded. "There's no way we're losing him."

Leroux wanted to share her confidence, but they were operating with limited resources. Normally, he'd task at least one satellite to help, but Morrison had nixed the idea. With the Russians being blamed for a state sanctioned nerve agent attack on foreign soil, there was no way they wouldn't notice a satellite retasked over Moscow at the same time a priority target was breaking out of prison.

They'd blame the United States for it, then claim America was rescuing their asset who had stolen the Novichok and used it to embarrass the Russian government.

This world is a mess.

"Something's happening."

Leroux leaned closer and cursed. "Here we go."

Leaving Pechatniki Pre-trial Detention Center

Moscow, Russia

"Are you okay?"

Grekov flinched at the driver's question. Sergei had been a colleague and friend for as long as he could remember, and he had a feeling they were partnered for a reason. They knew each other, and the brass likely felt they would never betray each other.

If only they knew.

He shifted in the passenger seat, risking a quick glance at his friend. "Yeah, it's just my stomach. It's been bothering me all morning."

"Nerves or drink?"

Grekov grunted. "Probably a little of both. I have to lay off the vodka."

Sergei laughed. "We both do. You need to find yourself a new wife. How long has it been since you lost Olga? Five years? The kids are all grown up and on their own. That apartment of yours is too empty."

Grekov frowned. His friend was right. He was painfully lonely, the bar an excuse to be surrounded by real people, though he interacted with them rarely, instead sitting in his corner booth in silence, merely staring at his glass or out the window at the people with far more interesting lives than his.

I'm so lonely!

"I have my cats."

"The worst kind of pet out there. They only love you when they need to be fed, and if you die, they'll eat *you.* You need a dog, my friend."

Grekov grunted. "Dogs are too much work."

"They're worth it."

"So are cats."

"I guess we'll agree to disagree."

"I guess."

His voice must have been a little too muted for Sergei to ignore. "Something really is bothering you, isn't it?"

They turned, their journey almost halfway over, and Grekov wondered if his fears were unjustified. "I'm just thinking of the future. Retirement."

Sergei grunted. "I know. Me too. Sometimes I wish I wasn't an honest cop. Can you imagine how much money we'd have stashed away now if we had only taken some of those bribes?"

Grekov's stomach flipped and the blood drained from his cheeks.

And Sergei noticed. "Hey, I was only joking."

"I know."

Sergei stared at him for a moment, and Grekov turned his head to face his side window, eyeballing a man on a motorcycle, wondering what type of idiot rode one at this time of year.

"Don't tell me…"

Sergei didn't finish his sentence, instead leaving his statement dangling, hoping, Grekov was sure, that his friend of so long would complete it for him, complete it in a way that didn't mean he had betrayed everything they both stood for.

"I-I did something stupid."

"Moriz, what did you do?"

Another motorcycle.

"I-I can't say."

A hand gripped his shoulder. "Tell me! Did you sell us out?"

Tears welled in Grekov's eyes. "I'm not sure."

"What the hell does that mean?"

"I thought he was his brother. I thought he just wanted to say goodbye."

Sergei cursed and grabbed the mike as two engines revved behind them, the distinct whine of motorcycles rapidly approaching. Grekov leaned closer to the window, staring at the sideview mirror, and nearly vomited at the sight of two motorcycles racing up the convoy, the riders slapping what had to be explosives to each of the vehicles.

Sergei spotted them too. "What's going on?"

Grekov closed his eyes, his secret already out, his worst fears confirmed. It was over for him, but perhaps he might save the others. "Call it in! We're under attack!"

Sergei dropped the mike, instead gripping the steering wheel with both hands as he jerked it to the left then the right. Grekov smiled as the motorcycle coming up his side swerved to avoid the rear end, slamming into a parked police unit, the streets from the jail to the courthouse closed and locked down for their journey only moments before they left.

Police surrounded the downed rider, but Grekov's focus had already turned to the other motorcycles racing up the sides, at least two more on his side, spiked tires visibly tearing up the winter road.

"How many can you see?" he asked, and Sergei stole a quick glance. "At least three on my side. You?"

"Two more."

Sergei swung again but two raced past them, giving them a wide berth, slapping their charges on the lead vehicles, the radios crackling with shouted calls for backup.

Then the worst horror Grekov could have imagined hit all at once.

The vehicles ahead erupted in flames as the explosives detonated simultaneously. Sergei slammed on the brakes so they wouldn't run into the rear of the now torn apart vehicle they had been following, and bile flooded Grekov's mouth as he caught sight of the trailing vehicles ablaze, some of the occupants who had survived the initial detonations struggling to escape the infernos as the support units and public lining the streets stood by in shock.

"We have to get out of here!" cried Sergei, downshifting then hammering on the gas as he cranked the wheel, taking them around the infernos blocking their path. "What did you do? What did you do?"

But Grekov couldn't speak. He leaned forward and vomited, his insides heaving out the horror of what he had done, the guilt of his betrayal, and the knowledge they were all about to die.

And instead of facing his inevitable future like a man, he openly wept as one of his few friends tried to save them both.

Boykov smiled at the sight. It had been so long since he had seen any action, his old heart was pounding with the adrenaline rush. Even in the height of his career, he had never participated in an operation like this. He was an assassin. He would man the lonely post, waiting for his target to appear, then take the single shot that would change history.

Never had he worked on something like this.

I think I chose the wrong profession.

This was action to the extreme, with no concerns for collateral damage, no concerns with body count, no worries about the consequences. This was an all-out assault to achieve a single outcome, no matter what the cost.

It was almost overwhelming.

And he was so happy he had insisted he be part of it.

He had no intention of getting in on the action. He was too old for that. He recognized the fact this type of operation was a young man's game. But he couldn't risk Minkin not holding up his end of the bargain and meeting with him.

He didn't trust the man.

After all, he was former KGB, and KGB were never to be trusted.

Including himself.

Their SUV pulled out in front of the escaping vehicle carrying their target, all four doors opening as the team of hired guns took aim, one with some sort of EMP weapon, something Boykov hadn't even known existed until this morning's briefing. A trigger was squeezed, and the power source it was connected to, sitting in the rear of their vehicle, sent a pulse into their target, killing its electronics and bringing it to a slow halt barely feet from them.

The team rushed forward, those that remained on the motorcycles taking up position around the operation, providing cover as they sprayed bursts of gunfire over the heads of the local police and civilians scattering for their lives.

Small charges were placed on all the doors, including the cab, and quickly detonated, the driver and passenger hauled out and thrown to the ground as the rear doors blasted open, a hail of gunfire from inside greeting the team.

Yet he wasn't paying attention to what was happening at the rear of the vehicle anymore, his entire attention now on the passenger, prone on the ground, a gun swinging toward his head as the driver was executed.

There would be no witnesses, apparently.

"Wait!" Boykov struggled out of the back seat and stumbled toward the passenger, his executioner staring back at him.

"Stay in the vehicle. That was the agreement."

"He's mine. He's seen my face."

Grekov twisted his head, his eyes wide with terror, his face the sickly pale of a guilty man. Boykov aimed his weapon at the poor bastard and his executioner relinquished his task to the elderly spy, quickly leaving to assist those at the rear. Boykov took a knee, pressing the barrel of his Makarov against the man's temple.

"I'm sorry it happened this way. I didn't know."

Tears rolled from Grekov's eyes and onto the frozen ground. "Just get it over with."

"Very well." He leaned in closer, lowering his voice. "Enjoy your retirement, my friend." He squeezed off two rounds, pressing the poor man's face into the pavement, making sure he wasn't moving, then headed back to the SUV, his heart hammering at the first shots he had taken in years.

Two shots that affected him more than all those that had preceded them.

Minkin tried to keep his cool as the armored transport rocked from multiple detonations, the four officers locked inside with him in a panic as they readied their weapons, the doors to the rear now hanging off their hinges, his rescuers wisely placing explosives on all points of weakness at once.

Gunfire erupted from all four defenders and he ducked, squeezing his eyes shut and covering his ears, preparing for what he suspected was about to happen. There was no way his men would fire inside the vehicle, not unless it became absolutely necessary.

But there was one thing they could do.

The flashbang thundered within the confined space, his own cries joining the unprepared others as their senses were overwhelmed by the device. The vehicle rocked as his men rushed in, gunfire erupting, all four defenders eliminated within seconds. Everything was a blur, his ears ringing, his eyes blinded with a kaleidoscope of colors, but he could still feel. Hands grabbed him and hauled him into an upright position, shadows moving about as orders were shouted, none of which he could make out.

Suddenly his wrists were freed of his restraints, then his ankles, and he was hauled to his feet and carried by both arms out of the vehicle, the harsh cold of a Moscow winter greeting him as his feet hit the ground, his vision and hearing slowly returning as he was shoved into the back of a waiting vehicle.

The whine of motorcycles and the engine of his getaway vehicle were the first sounds he could distinguish, and he was pressed into his seat as they accelerated. He rubbed his eyes then turned to see the man he least expected sitting beside him, smiling.

Boykov.

"Feel like sharing now?"

Grekov lay on the frozen ground, not moving a muscle, his ears still ringing from the two shots his betrayer had fired into the pavement only inches from his head. And as he lay there, playing dead, listening to his comrades dying around him, their murderers escaping the scene only minutes later, he shook from the cold and the shame.

He had lived, yet he feared none of the others had.

And it was all his fault.

Why did he let me live?

What was it he had said?

I'm sorry it happened this way. I didn't know.

To have let him live must mean some level of remorse. The man had to be feeling guilty about how things had turned out, though there was no way he could feel as guilty as Grekov felt right now.

This was all his fault.

A tear rolled down his nose and onto the pavement.

Nobody knows except Sergei.

He opened his eyes, and gasped at the first thing he saw. Sergei, lying dead, on the opposite side of the vehicle, his bloody head visible under the raised undercarriage.

And guilt racked him at the relief he felt.

Nobody knows.

If he managed to survive the day, he could use the money to get out of Russia, to begin a new life, and to try and make up for what he had done here today.

He pushed to his feet as the crowds of bystanders and police personnel guarding the route finally found the courage to approach the scene, and he drew a slow breath, trying to steady himself.

As he was surrounded, questions bombarding him, cellphones held out and recording him, he realized there would be no escaping what had happened.

He was the one that lived.

And there was no reason for it.

And there was no way his faked execution wasn't caught on someone's camera.

He'd be arrested before the day was out, his children arrested to make him talk, and he'd spend the rest of his life rotting in prison.

Why didn't you just kill me?

He closed his eyes, a long sigh escaping, then reached for his weapon. Several in the crowd screamed as he drew his gun, those gathered quickly backing away, then gasping collectively as he squeezed the trigger.

Finishing the job the man who had betrayed him should have.

Off-the-books Operations Center

Outside Bethesda, Maryland

Tommy's shoulders trembled as tears rolled down his cheeks. Leroux wanted to reach out to comfort the poor kid, but there was an op underway, and there was no time. All he could do was offer a steadying hand on that shaking shoulder, and a calm voice.

"Tell me you've got that vehicle locked."

Sonya nodded, her experience winning out over emotion. "I do. As long as the drone holds out, we'll know where they went."

Leroux frowned, glancing at the indicator showing how much battery power was left. This was a miniature drone, not designed for high speed and long deployments. For the moment, it was keeping up thanks to the fact it was above the fray, not dealing with the traffic the escape vehicle now found itself in.

Tommy sniffed, wiping his tears away with the back of his hand. "They-they're going to have to switch vehicles soon, right?"

Leroux nodded. "I would. Every cop in the city is looking for them."

Sonya pointed. "There go the motorcycles."

Leroux watched as they all split off in different directions, chewing his cheek as he watched them make tight turns on slippery roads. "They must be using studded tires."

Sonya agreed. "That's the only explanation. Should we try and track them?"

Leroux shook his head. "Forget them, they're not important. Let the Russians deal with them." He activated his comm. "Romeo One, this is Control Actual, come in."

Kane immediately responded. "Go ahead, Control."

"Are you getting our tracking information?"

"Yup. I'm a couple of streets over. Don't worry about me."

"Copy that. We're expecting them to exchange vehicles, somewhere out of sight, probably a camera dead zone."

"That makes sense. Tommy, any chance you can find that zone?"

Tommy sniffed. "I-I'll try." The kid attacked his keyboard. Keeping busy was the best way to push through. The true collapse would come later when he was alone with his thoughts. Leroux hated the fact he was so used to this type of carnage, and quite often he was the one directing the killing, which made it even more difficult, though in situations like this, where he was a mere witness to the events, there was a sense of helplessness that could become overwhelming if left unchecked.

The kid might not be cut out for this line of work.

That was fine. Most weren't. The CIA conducted extensive screening before anyone was thrust into the situation Tommy had been, and Leroux was regretting having agreed to Kane's suggestion the young man be added to the team to help out. He had agreed to the addition for selfish reasons. Yet were they selfish? Yes, it would mean they could work alternating shifts with a pair always active, reducing the workload and stress level, but no one had thought anything like this would happen. No one had thought there'd be a massacre of this proportion executed on the streets of Moscow, while they watched it all happen, taking no action to prevent it.

And perhaps that was what was troubling him. They had known this would happen, and they had done nothing. How many lives had been lost today because they had kept the intel to themselves? How many could they have saved with a simple phone call? Was Morrison's life worth so many? Was one man worth the dozens lost?

The secure phone rang and he answered it. "Yes?"

"Should any further intel come into our possession that could save lives, we share it. Understood?"

Leroux hesitated before responding to his new mission parameters from Morrison. He had been monitoring remotely as well, so had witnessed everything they had, and no doubt was asking the same questions as the rest of them. "But, sir, that could put your life at risk."

"You have your orders."

The phone went dead and he dropped into his seat, exhaling deeply, his stomach in knots, as it would be his job to share the intel, and should it lead to Morrison's death, he'd be the one who would have to live with that for the rest of his life.

Sometimes I hate this job.

Over Moscow, Russia

Natasha Ivashin's uncle had been absolutely correct. By using his recommended methods, panic had been created by those involved, and Minkin had done what she needed. He had his people break him out of jail. There was no way she could get to him on the inside, but now that he was out, there was at least the possibility.

You should have finished him when you had the chance.

She had failed in his office, though only because of the police raid. If the alarm hadn't distracted her, she would have succeeded, she was certain. But now she was being given a second chance, as long as she didn't lose him. Uncle Cheslav had provided her with the time of the transfer, and a drone provided by him had done the rest.

It was a brutal attack, with dozens dead, but that wasn't her concern, and she wasn't responsible. Though deep down, she knew she was. After all, he was probably arrested because he had supplied the Novichok—the timing of the raid was simply too coincidental. If her uncle had never requested it, it never would have been stolen, Minkin never would have been arrested, and there never would have been an escape costing dozens of innocent lives.

Yet she still didn't care.

She had never really cared about anything. It was why she had excelled at mixed martial arts, and why she had ultimately been kicked out of her gym—she just couldn't stop delivering the beating. Once the adrenaline flowed, once the trigger was pulled, nothing would stop her.

Knocking out a ref after beating her opponent an inch from death was the final straw, and she had been banned. Anger management courses, provided through her uncle, had never found the root of the problem, as she would never reveal her true feelings.

Whenever she was in a situation that triggered an adrenaline rush, she nearly blacked out with the rage that ensued, images of her dead father consuming her, whatever was in her way instantly becoming responsible for her loss.

It affected her love life, where sex became a contest to win, with some of her partners initially turned on by her aggressiveness, though all eventually coming to fear and loathe it, leaving her in short order. It had affected her friendships, with any perceived slight resulting in verbal and often physical confrontations that quickly ended any hopes at reconciliation. And it affected her professional life for all the same reasons.

Until she had been given some coping tools. The mental exercises provided by the counselor had worked, at least enough for her to complete her degree and become a teacher, her uncle making sure her past record had been cleaned up when any background checks were done.

I owe him everything.

He was the only good thing in her life, now that her mother was dead. She would never have a lover or friends. She simply couldn't risk being triggered again. Today, with everything being recorded, an altercation would hit the Internet within minutes, and her career would be over, and then she'd have nothing.

She did enjoy the children. Perhaps it was because they looked up to her unconditionally, though there were the brats. But they were kids, and for some reason, she could control her outbursts with them. Teaching did bring joy to her heart, joy she had only experienced in her moments of victory until then. And with her students, every day had its small victories, and every day made her feel a little better because of it.

Yet all her progress, all her years of hard work, had unraveled with the death of her mother, the revelation of the letter from her father, and the bombshell dropped on her by her uncle.

Her father was KGB, had attempted to assassinate Gorbachev in a bid to preserve one of the most evil empires to have ever existed, and he had killed himself to protect her and her mother.

And those responsible were still out there, enjoying their lives these past thirty years.

It enraged her, every moment since, one of tortuous fury she saw no way of coming back from.

She was consumed with hate, hate she could use to accomplish her goals, but hate she knew would ultimately lead to her downfall.

And she didn't care.

She tapped a key on her laptop, transferring the second down payment on the contract.

"Payment received. The rest is due upon completion."

She snapped shut the laptop. "The funds are already allotted. A third-party will transfer them the moment they receive confirmation."

"Understood. We will execute the contract within the agreed upon time frame. Contact me if you need anything further."

"I will." She ended the call, turning her attention to a tablet computer, the tracking drone indicating the final destination of Minkin. She turned to the pilot of the helicopter she was in, hovering over the general vicinity. "You've got the location?"

He nodded. "Moving in now."

She braced as they banked to the left, then grabbed the PKP Pecheneg machine gun provided her by Uncle Cheslav. She had been training on it for weeks, her uncle, fortunately, having introduced her to guns at an early age. They didn't intimidate her, and she had always enjoyed their feel in her hands.

Especially something as powerful as this.

Minkin was about to die in a most satisfying way.

Six men in the room. One dead the day of, her father shortly after, Boykov eliminated in the explosion, Minkin about to die, an unknown American, and a sixth man her uncle was hard at work identifying.

Plus the two who had foiled the plot, one dying, the other soon to be dead.

She was making progress, and today would see the end of another.

I will avenge you, Father.

Approaching Ulitsa Pererva Parking Garage

Moscow, Russia

"Tell me everything."

Minkin eyed Boykov for a moment as their vehicle continued to jerk left and right, the driver expertly guiding them through Moscow traffic. There wasn't much time before they would undoubtedly switch vehicles, as every minute they remained in this truck placed them at risk as word spread across the city of what had just happened.

And the moment they switched vehicles, his association with Boykov would be over.

"What do you want to know?"

"I want to know who the hell is trying to kill me."

"Some woman, is my understanding."

"But who is she?"

"She's the niece of Cheslav Aristov. That's all I know."

"Niece? Why the hell does she want to kill us?"

"I have no idea."

"Is it her uncle who wants us dead, and he's using her to do it?"

Minkin shrugged. "I don't know, but I doubt it. He's powerful enough to use professionals, not family."

Boykov frowned. "Then it has to be something else. Who was in the room?"

Minkin shook his head. "You know as much as I know. There were six men with no names."

"Let's narrow it down. We were both there, and we're obviously not trying to kill ourselves. You ordered me after the meeting to kill our agent who was going to let me in the building, which I did. That leaves three. Who was the American?"

"I don't know. All I know was that he was CIA and trusted. And he did his part. I also know the KGB agent assigned to the CIA agent who tried to stop you, was the target of the Novichok attack in England. His name is Igor Kulick."

Boykov's eyebrows shot up. "I didn't know. So that means whoever is behind this knows more than those who were only in that room. I had no idea about him until just now." His eyes narrowed. "How did *you* know?"

"Because I had to clean up the mess after the fact. I led the team that cleaned up the bodies, and saved your life, I might add."

Boykov eyed him. "It sounds to me like you were in charge."

Minkin shook his head. "No, it was only meant to look that way. I was following orders."

"Whose orders?"

"I don't know."

"Were they in the room?"

Minkin hesitated. He knew more than he was saying, though not much. Fear was probably the motivating factor in keeping him silent, yet did it matter? He was about to disappear where no one could ever find him. Did he really need to keep the secret he had held for so many years any longer?

He regarded Boykov for a moment. The man was old, older than him, and he sensed no fear whatsoever. His motivation was clear. Self-preservation. And would having a man like this, out there trying to stop whoever was behind this, be a bad thing? If he did succeed in eliminating the guilty party, then life might be a little less stressful.

"Sir, we're here."

Minkin peered out the windows to see they were inside a parking garage, another vehicle idling nearby as the doors were opened. He stepped outside, Boykov following. He was led by the arm to the waiting vehicle, the door already open, new personnel inside. He turned to Boykov. "Yes, the man who gave me my orders was in the room."

"And he selected me to be the shooter?"

"Yes."

"Did you really know any of what was going on?"

Minkin grunted. "I had been briefed the day before. I knew almost nothing, and expected to be eliminated myself."

"Why didn't they?"

"I think they wanted someone to blame if it ever came to light. They certainly made it look like I was in charge, didn't they?"

Boykov nodded, his lips pursed. "I certainly thought so."

"Exactly. But I'll let you in on a little secret, not that it will help you, since we don't know their names. The one who briefed me?"

"Yes?"

Gunfire erupted, multiple shots in rapid succession blasting apart the concrete where they stood. Minkin dove in the back of the idling vehicle and it peeled away, leaving Boykov and the rest behind. He spun in his seat, staring out the rear window as he watched Boykov collapse, gripping his chest, the rest of his team, weapons drawn, attempting to find the shooter as they were torn apart.

Suddenly, those that remained began firing in the same direction, their target located.

Natasha continued to fire, her blood boiling at the sight of the still breathing Boykov. How the bastard had survived the collapse of an entire apartment building while living on the top floor was beyond her, yet there he stood, as plain as day, without a scratch on him.

And her plan had changed.

Boykov was a nobody. He could disappear into the woodwork and never be found again. In fact, she had no idea how Uncle Cheslav had managed to find him in the first place, but finding him again might prove impossible.

Minkin, on the other hand, was probably the most wanted man in Russia now. He'd likely be captured at some point by the authorities, and she could target him again.

So, she had shot Boykov, and put several more bullets into his body just to make sure.

The helicopter banked away as what remained of Minkin's team finally spotted her, the open air parking garage having provided her with a clean shot, and the powerful weapon the distance to leave the chopper unnoticed long enough for her to find her target.

She packed up her weapon and sent a message to her uncle on the secure tablet.

And he replied immediately.

I've found the American. I've sent you instructions. Good luck.

Off-the-books Operations Center

Outside Bethesda, Maryland

"Track that helicopter!"

Sonya's fingers hovered over her keyboard. "I can't."

Leroux spun toward her. "What do you mean?"

"All we've got is the drone. It can't keep up with a helicopter."

Leroux cursed. "How much time do we have before the batteries die?"

"Maybe ten minutes."

He sighed. "Fine, but monitor the feeds for anything on that helicopter."

"Yes, sir."

Leroux dropped into his seat. From the video they had managed to capture on their drone, it appeared someone in a helicopter had shot Boykov, and Minkin had escaped in a new vehicle. It made no sense. Why would they target Boykov? And why was Boykov even there? Were he and Minkin working together? That made no sense either. Minkin was a billionaire, and Boykov was a destitute pensioner. There was no way those two were working together. But Boykov was the shooter, and Minkin had given the briefing on the operation. It made sense that Minkin would know who Boykov was, even if no names had been used.

But why was Minkin being targeted? If he gave the briefing, didn't that mean he was in charge? Wouldn't he have the most to lose if the plot were to come to light? Killing Boykov made sense, and killing Minkin only would if he weren't actually the one in charge.

His eyes widened slightly. If Minkin wasn't in charge, then it had to be one of the other two men in the room. It made no sense why they were there, as they didn't seem to have done anything. Minkin seemed to be directing things, Boykov was the shooter, West was responsible for commandeering the American frequencies, and the other unknown subject was in charge of getting Boykov into the building to take the shot.

What were the other two men doing? They had to be there for a reason, yet they appeared to have no assignment.

They had to be the brains behind it.

Perhaps not the brains, but the men in charge.

One of them has to be behind this.

His eyes widened at a thought. This woman was the right age to have had a father that was involved. They had managed to determine she had no uncle, but her father had been a major in the KGB. He could have been in the room that day, he could be one of the two unidentified men.

He rolled his chair closer to Tommy. "Send the files we have on Major Ivashin to Agent West. Let's see if he recognizes the man."

Third Ring Road

Moscow, Russia

Kane gunned the engine, shooting down the shoulder of the road, horns honking in annoyance as he blazed a trail toward the offramp that should let him intercept his target. It hadn't been hard to determine what vehicle Minkin had transferred to—it was the one blasting through the gate at the parking garage while gunfire took its toll overhead.

Leroux's team had retasked the drone to follow it, but time was running out on the small device. He was questioning Morrison's decision to keep this within the family, despite the CIA now cleared of involvement, and the only thing he could think of was that the man felt guilty about what had happened so long ago.

And he understood the guilt. Morrison had kept his mouth shut. Perhaps if he hadn't, perhaps if he had told his handlers what had happened, those involved could have been apprehended, and the innocents now dead would still be alive.

But hindsight was always 20/20, and there was no point living in the rearview mirror. Kane as well had done it for too long, blaming himself for a mission gone terribly wrong where women and children had been killed. It hadn't been his fault. There was no way he could have known, but he had watched it unfold in horrifying clarity through his scope, and had blamed himself for years, drinking himself into oblivion whenever possible, living a life of debauchery when not on duty.

Fang had changed all that. He had confronted his demons and was pushing through them, though his dreams were still on occasion haunted by what he had seen that day.

And he wondered if Morrison was now a haunted man.

Whatever the man might be feeling, he was compromising the mission by not bringing in a full team and the entire resources of the Agency to bear.

"Take a left immediately after you clear the offramp, then an immediate right. That should put you ahead of them."

"Copy that."

He was thankful Sonya Tong was on the team. She was excellent in these situations, and was a huge asset to his buddy, who while the best at what he did, couldn't do everything himself. He executed the turns, hammering on the gas as he surged ahead.

"Okay, traffic is clear. They're half a mile out from your position. Do whatever it is you're going to do."

"Copy that."

He kept the accelerator floored, the target vehicle in sight ahead, then hammered on his brakes, bringing him to a shuddering halt as he cranked the wheel, blocking both lanes. The target SUV came to a halt only feet from him, four men jumping out, guns drawn as he exited the vehicle, his hands raised.

"Tell Mr. Minkin that his representative from the insurance company would like to talk to him."

This surprised the men enough to not shoot, and words were exchanged with someone in the back seat. The guard stepped back and Minkin climbed out, a slight smile on his face.

"So, you're the man Svetlana talked of."

"I am. She's quite the woman. I would have assumed you'd be taking her with you."

He chuckled as he strode slowly toward Kane. "She'll be sent for, don't you worry. A woman like that, well, you don't let get away."

Kane smiled. "I agree." He ended the pleasantries. "We're both in a hurry, so I'll cut to the chase. I need to know who arranged your meeting to hand over the Novichok. I need to know the name of her uncle."

"And why should I tell you?"

"Because they're also targeting a friend of mine, and I intend to stop them. If I succeed, then you'll be able to rest a little easier."

Minkin nodded slowly. "This is true. But I think the young lady who tried to kill me won't be stopped by killing her uncle, nor am I certain he's behind this."

"Then there's no harm in giving me his name."

"Nor is there any in giving me hers."

Kane thought for a moment, and only for a moment. She was a murderer, and deserved no protection from him. "Her name is Natasha Ivashin."

"Interesting. It means nothing to me. I had hoped I might recognize it. It might have explained a few things."

"And the name of the uncle?"

Minkin regarded him for a moment. "Surely, if you know her name, you can figure that out yourself?"

Kane shook his head. "She has no uncle."

Minkin's eyebrows rose. "Very interesting. Now, why lie about that?" He tapped his chin. "I'm going to give you the name, American, as long as you tell me one thing."

Kane frowned. "And what's that?"

"Who do you work for?"

Kane smiled slightly. "I told you, I'm with your insurance company."

Minkin chuckled. "Bullshit. You've got Agency written all over you."

"If you're so sure, why bother asking."

"I just wanted to be certain." He turned, heading back to his vehicle and his impatient security detail. He glanced back at Kane. "The man you're looking for is Cheslav Aristov." He began to climb inside when he paused. "And CIA, be careful. He's a powerful man."

"Thank you." Kane held up a finger. "One more thing."

"What?"

"You gave the briefing, but you weren't in charge, were you?"

"No."

"Do you know who was?"

"I don't know his name, but he was in the room. Figure out who everyone was, and you'll figure out who's behind all this."

Minkin shut the door and Kane climbed back in his vehicle, Minkin's already steering past him, the few cars blocked, too scared to honk their horns with all the guns on display, inching past. And as he headed back toward central Moscow, a smile spread.

They finally had a name that might lead somewhere.

Natasha Ivashin Residence

Moscow, Russia

Viktor Zorkin pushed open the rear door to the humble home, its World War Two era plaster cracked and failing on the back, all efforts to maintain respectability reserved for the front, a little of the apparently limited funds left for the sides. It was so typical of the area, and so sad. Everyone tried to make it appear as if things were good, at least on the outside, but the reality was far from different.

People were hurting.

Sanctions coupled with a government out of control on military spending, along with corruption at unparalleled levels that had their glorious leader's net worth pegged north of $50 billion and possibly as high as $200 billion, were reminding him of the collapse of the Soviet Union, when the communist-run government spent itself into bankruptcy trying to keep up with the faked American Star Wars program.

It had been a masterstroke of deception, and he tipped his hat to his former foe for the victory.

But today, all fault lay with their own leadership, and he saw no end in sight short of an assassin's bullet.

Here we are, thirty years later, and assassination is still the only answer?

If Boykov had succeeded, what would the world have been like? A hardliner would have taken over the Communist Party, there would have been a purge of anyone that had supported glasnost and perestroika, and the population would have been rallied to support the renewal of the Iron Curtain.

And perhaps there might have been the war to truly end all wars.

And today, should someone eliminate their glorious leader, what would happen? Would their once fledgling democracy be allowed to flourish once again? Would another hardliner take over? Would the military stage a coup? Would the egoist's foreign policy be put to an end so peace between the two "sides" might finally be achieved?

He had no idea, nor did he care to speculate. That wasn't his problem anymore. It wasn't his generation's problem anymore. It was up to the youth of the nation to chart its future, and so far, with their support of the current leadership, he held out little hope. They were allowing themselves to be brainwashed by a former KGB colonel, and deserved whatever they got.

He closed the door behind him, the heavy closed curtains plunging him into darkness. He left the lights off, instead relying upon a pair of night vision goggles he now slipped over his eyes. The house was empty, of that he was certain—Natasha Ivashin had just murdered Boykov and half of Minkin's team. He didn't have a problem with that, especially the killing of Minkin's team—they had just slaughtered dozens of innocent police. As for Boykov, the man had lived far longer than one in his line of work normally did, and probably was pleased to die in a hail of gunfire, rather than in some lonely apartment, gripping a bottle of vodka and a pistol.

He would have liked to have seen Minkin buy it. Anyone who would give up Novichok to save his own skin didn't deserve to share the same air with its possible victims. But Kane's message from only minutes ago, indicated Minkin's survival had borne at least one positive thing.

They now knew who the uncle was, and he had little doubt the CIA was pulling every piece of information they could while he tried to discover more about Natasha and her possible motivations.

He was in the kitchen at the back of the house, a dated affair that was tidy though neglected, half a rotting loaf of bread reeking of mold. He made quick work of the room, finding nothing of interest, then moved into the main living area of the home, a single room at the front of the house, all the curtains drawn, nothing out of place beyond a box of tissues, a handful crumpled up on a side table where someone had obviously sat in tears.

He opened the drawers on an antique rolltop desk sitting in the corner, probably worth more to some collector than the rest of the contents of the home, and riffled through the papers there, finding nothing of interest. With no other possibilities of paperwork in the room, he turned his attention to the mantle over a fireplace home to a dozen framed pictures. Their suspect was featured in several of them at varying ages, her smiles forced or missing in all but the few of her as a tiny child.

Probably before her father killed himself.

There were several of the man in question, most in Soviet-era uniform, but one stood out. He was smiling with another man, both with their arms around each other, both in KGB uniforms. Happier times, and perhaps someone close to the man who might be identifiable. He took photos of all pictures on the mantle, sending them to Kane's team, then headed up the narrow stairs to the second floor.

The master bedroom had nothing beyond a few more photos and some personal documents belonging to the late mother, the lone bathroom, of course, had nothing, but the second bedroom, clearly Natasha's, revealed a treasure trove of information in a single document.

A letter, sitting open on her nightstand, written by hand and dated over thirty years ago, her father's signature on the bottom.

And its contents explained almost everything if it were only recently opened, which he suspected, the paper and the envelope that had contained it in far too pristine condition for three decades of handling.

It was her father's suicide note, addressed to her, clearly meant for when she was older, explaining that he had been involved in something he described as shameful, which Zorkin thought was an interesting way of describing it. He would have thought the man would be proud of what he had tried to do, though it was dated several years after the attempt, so perhaps he had changed his mind in the aftermath.

His reason for killing himself was also interesting, even more so than his characterization of the plot. He had taken his life to protect his family from what he feared might happen in the future. That suggested he was concerned someone would get to him through his family, and by killing himself, had felt he would eliminate that motivation in his enemies.

But who were his enemies? Konstantin Ivashin was a major in the KGB, and Kane's team had determined that Minkin was only a captain. If Ivashin were in the room, which they still didn't know if he was, then he would have outranked Minkin. But if he had enemies, it meant there were others that might want to kill him, others who likely outranked him.

Could it be the sixth man? Did he fear him enough to take his own life? Would the sixth man have killed Ivashin's wife and daughter for revenge? To keep him silent? Or were there more involved beyond those in the room? It was possible. Definitely possible, though he suspected if there were any, they were few, as something like this would be kept to a tightknit group.

In fact, he suspected there might not be anyone else involved, for the mere fact Minkin was in the room, and apparently not in charge, if Kane's last message were to be believed. That meant one of the two men they had yet to identify was likely in charge, and he had a feeling one of them was Major Ivashin, and the other was his superior, for if he weren't, then who was Ivashin scared of?

Everyone involved was in that room.

It was the only explanation that made sense. The senior man was probably a colonel, perhaps a lieutenant colonel, and a control freak. Most at that level in the KGB were. He would want to make sure every single instruction was relayed properly and in its entirety, and a micromanager like that would need to be in the room, even if he remained silent. If anything was missed or inaccurate, he would, after the fact, tell his second-in-command, a major like Ivashin, who would then correct things.

Or pass on secondary commands, like the command West hadn't heard in the room to kill the guard at the door, a command obviously given to Boykov after the fact.

And the target, another thing not mentioned in the meeting.

It all made sense when thought of from that perspective. A commanding officer who had to control every aspect of an operation. A trusted second-in-command like Ivashin, who could be used as a fall guy should it become necessary, and to pass on any secondary orders so the man in command could deny ever giving any such orders. A handpicked assassin known to have issues with the reforms, then his removal from the KGB orchestrated with the rumors spread about why he had been forced out. A poor expendable to be used to let the assassin into the building to make the shot. And an American, added at the last minute, allowing them to solidify the frameup taking place.

A small, contained unit, with no one on the outside to let the details slip. A unit small enough to eliminate after the fact with little effort, should it become necessary.

He liked it. It made sense. It was clean.

Except for one thing.

Why now? Why thirty years later? He could understand the daughter wanting revenge if she were off her rocker, but she had to be getting the information from somewhere. There was no way she could discover by herself who was involved, which meant she had a source, and it could only be the sixth man.

Zorkin's eyebrows shot up.

Could the uncle be the sixth man?

It had to be, yet it couldn't. Why would Natasha's father fear him? Why would he kill himself to save the lives of his family? Cheslav Aristov had to be close to Natasha and her mother. A girl didn't call a man her uncle when he wasn't, unless they were close. And for him to help her now, to use his connections to procure a nerve agent as deadly as Novichok, he had to care for her very deeply.

And for her father.

Was he too seeking revenge? That made sense.

He smiled, his jaw slowly dropping.

His good friend, Natasha's father, told him everything before he killed himself. Aristov wasn't involved, but knew everything he did because his good friend, his friend so close that his daughter called him uncle, told him everything. And if Ivashin were the second-in-command of the operation, he likely would have handpicked Minkin, the shooter Boykov, and the guard Boykov was ordered to kill. Ivashin would have been recruited himself, probably by the sixth man, so he would know who that was. And as the second-in-command, he likely would have been responsible for the cleanup after the fact, so would have discovered that Kulick and Morrison were the agents who had helped foil their plans.

But how was West brought in?

He chewed his cheek for a moment, then shook his head. The weapon purchase made through his old rival would have been done through standard channels. Things like that were done all the time, and no one would think twice about being given an order to purchase the weapon and deliver it to a drop point, none of the five already involved revealed to those handling the deal. West's request to join would have been passed on, the mystery man in command would have approved it as he intended to frame the Americans, and West would have been brought in and used as the fall guy.

Alex was supposed to die.

According to West's account of what happened that day, and the briefing he had read on Morrison's version, Boykov wasn't surprised that he was there.

It's about time.

That's what Morrison's summary indicated Boykov had said. That meant Boykov was expecting West to show up, and Boykov was probably supposed to kill him after completing the mission, plant West's fingerprints on the rifle, then play the hero in eliminating the evil American who had just killed the Soviet people's beloved leader.

He grunted, shaking his head. It was an extremely well thought out plan, and if West hadn't played them, it would have succeeded brilliantly, he was sure.

He took a photo of the letter, sending it to Kane's team, then folded it up, placing it back in the envelope and tucking it into his pocket. He headed down the stairs and out the back, what to do next running through his head.

The uncle knows everything.

But how could they possibly get him to admit he was involved in a conspiracy that had brought huge international pressure against the government he now served in?

He paused, a chill racing up and down his spine.

If he knows everything, then he knows who Alex is.

And if Cheslav Aristov had managed to track down Minkin, Boykov, and Kulick, it suggested he might have the resources to track down his friend.

He pulled out his phone, firing a warning message to West.

Alex West Residence

Black Forest, Germany

West's frown continued to deepen as he stared at the love of his life, and their daughter. Adelle was still as beautiful in his eyes as she was the day he had first spotted her across the room in Moscow, decades ago, during the height of the Cold War. She was a spy working for France, a country that couldn't be trusted back then, its socialist government playing both sides too often.

Somehow, despite not trusting her one iota, there had been a connection, a few stress-reliever encounters that eventually blossomed into more, then enough to risk both their careers before she disappeared from his life for decades.

And reappeared with a daughter. *His* daughter, Alexis, now a member of France's clandestine services herself, following in her parents' footsteps. Though he felt he barely knew her, he loved her deeply, and was making an effort in his few remaining years to be the father she had never had, and to his delight, she seemed open to his overtures, though they'd never have the connection, the bond that decades of raising a child provided.

"I'm going to walk the perimeter."

If it were possible, he would have deepened his frown. "Just stay inside. Let the technology do its job. These are ballistic windows, and all the walls, including the roof and floors, have a thick layer of fiberglass sandwiched in between. Nothing short of a tank round is getting in here."

Alexis eyed him. "You of all people should know not to rely on technology."

He gave his daughter a look. "We *did* have technology back in the day. I'm not *that* old."

Alexis grinned. "That wasn't technology, that stuff was just one step above steampunk. Mama says that most of the stuff didn't work half the time."

West winked at Adelle. "That's because hers wasn't made in America." He waved his daughter away. "Fine, walk the perimeter, but make sure you put a vest on."

Alexis tapped her chest, the distinctive knock of a bullet-resistant vest echoing back. "Way ahead of you, Papa." She headed out the door and he sighed.

"I love it when she calls me that."

Adelle curled her legs up under her. "I told you she'd come around."

He smiled then wagged a finger at her. "I told you to stay away. I wish you'd listen to me sometimes."

"I'm too old to learn new tricks."

"What? The trick of avoiding assassin's bullets? I thought you mastered that years ago."

"I missed you, and no psychotic millennial is going to keep me from the man I love."

"So, you brought our daughter with you?"

"She insisted. And she's trained, with joints that don't ache." Adelle tilted her head toward him. "What, you're going to fight off some young woman who's been trained as an MMA fighter?" She grunted. "Now that's a fight I'd actually pay to see."

"I'd defeat her with my charm."

Adelle chuckled. "You don't have that much game, my love."

"I can still charm the pants off you."

She shrugged. "I've always been easy, you know that."

He grinned. "Thank God!" He held up the tablet with the latest briefing notes from Kane's team, another update expected soon. "My memory might be a little foggy, but Natasha Ivashin's father was definitely in the room. That means we know five of the six now. And if he was a major, and Minkin only a captain, then he might have been in command, though I doubt it. Like Viktor said last night when I spoke to him, why would he kill himself if he was in charge?"

"Do you have any idea who the sixth man could be?"

West shook his head. "None. I can barely remember what he looked like. I sat on the same side of the table as Ivashin and him, and Ivashin was between us. And the lighting was piss poor Soviet era garbage. Even thirty years ago, I doubt I could have picked him out of a lineup."

"That's unfortunate."

"Well, in situations like that, you don't exactly ask the guy sitting beside you to lean back so you can get a good look at the face of the coconspirator sitting beside him."

"That's the advantage of being a woman. I would have simply asked the man beside me to get me a drink of water, and he would have."

West grunted. "Magic lady bits do work wonders, though do you really think Soviet-era conspiracists would have agreed to an American female agent being involved?"

She frowned, her head slowly bobbing. "They were sexist pigs back then." She grunted. "Still are."

An alarm beeped and West tapped the notification on his tablet, a map of the area appearing showing a motion detector triggered at the perimeter.

"Trouble?"

"Somebody's tripped a sensor."

"Could it be Alexis?"

He shook his head. "No." His eyes narrowed, his heart fluttering with the implications of what he was looking at. "I don't see her at all on here!"

Natasha lay prone on the cold ground, a light dusting of snow covering the area as she lined up her shot. Her uncle had come through for her yet again, delivering her the American traitor's location, along with papers that would get her across the border, and plane tickets to Frankfurt.

And a weapon waiting for her when she arrived, sitting in the trunk of a rental.

She knew from the photos her uncle had been KGB, yet she had never expected him to still be so well connected. Was it his contacts from the old days, kept fresh over the years, or was it his new position that gave him access to the information necessary for her to succeed?

She suspected it was a little of both, with his money greasing the wheels when it became necessary.

She had no way to thank the man, beyond her love, though her success would perhaps repay some of the tremendous debt she now owed him. He had been equally upset with her discovery, her questions reminding him of something he had buried years ago. The very fact he was helping, demonstrated the rage he had suppressed with her father's suicide. Thirty years ago, there was likely nothing he could have done about it. He wasn't wealthy like he was now, and the Soviet Union and its successor was in turmoil.

But now he had the means, and she was providing the opportunity, both of them, together, avenging her father's death.

And in her scope, right now, sat the man who had betrayed them all. The man who had shot Boykov in the back, dooming the plot to failure, resulting in her father taking the blame from whoever was ultimately in charge, a man he feared enough to kill himself to protect her and her mother.

She watched Alex West for a moment as her rage built, his quaint little home nestled in the beautiful Black Forest equipped with a large window providing him with an unobstructed view of anyone approaching, and a clear shot for her. As the man laughed about something, she adjusted her aim and debated putting a hole in the head of the woman who he no doubt shared a life with, a happy life denied to her father.

But she resisted. The woman wasn't her target. She readjusted, positioning her finger on the trigger as she inhaled deeply, then slowly exhaled.

A twig snapped behind her and she rolled onto her back, swinging the rifle at the woman standing only feet away, a gun pointed directly at her.

"Natasha Ivashin, I presume?"

Natasha continued to swing the weapon, her mission over, there nothing left to lose. A shot rang out, her shoulder controlling the weapon jerking with the impact, her muscles spasming, the trigger squeezing.

But her shot went wide, her assailant rushing forward, yanking the weapon from her hands and tossing it to the side.

"Kill me."

The woman shook her head. "Maybe when my father is finished with you." She flicked her weapon. "Get up."

Natasha struggled to her feet, gripping her shoulder, debating whether she could still take the woman despite her wound. In the ring, she had no doubt. Even with a dislocated shoulder, she had defeated an opponent single-handed.

Though this one had a gun.

But I want to die.

She charged, rage roaring from within, and the woman stepped calmly aside, pistol whipping her on the back of the head as she passed, knocking her out cold in a humiliatingly easy defeat.

House on Mosfilmovskaya Apartments

Moscow, Russia

Kane fit the final tracker on Svetlana's luggage then hurried for the door. The woman was in the building's private gym, but he wasn't sure for how long, and he was concerned his clandestine entry into the building might be discovered despite Leroux's successful overriding of the security systems.

Something could have been missed, and his presence had to go undetected.

Minkin was still key, and they had to find him. Now that West had confirmed Natasha's father was one of the two unidentified men, they had to know if he was in charge. Minkin had said he knew which one was, he just didn't know the name. Kane suspected Ivashin wasn't in charge, otherwise he wouldn't have committed suicide out of fear of someone else coming along to clean up the mess.

But suspicions weren't proof.

Due to their limited resources, Leroux hadn't been able to track Minkin beyond their brief encounter, and Svetlana was their best hope. Minkin had suggested he'd be sending for her, the best squeeze the old man could hope for if what remained of his years were spent in hiding. Kane sensed Svetlana did care for the man to a point, certainly enough to continue living a life of luxury, even if it meant some changes to their situation. He suspected, however, that she'd eventually tire of life on the run, and would head back to Moscow to find another sugar daddy to take care of her.

After all, she had made it clear monogamy wasn't part of her game plan.

The door to the apartment clicked and Kane cursed, rushing back to the bedroom as Svetlana whipped into the apartment like a whirlwind, the sounds of bags, purses, heels and other items being tossed as she made her way inside.

What the hell do I do now?

He sighed.

You take a page out of the old playbook.

He silently entered her ensuite bathroom and turned on the shower, then yanked his top off, thankful he wasn't wearing a suit with a dress shirt.

"Hello? Is someone there?"

He hopped on the bed and slid under the covers, leaving his chest exposed, and struck as seductive a pose as he could manage. "It's me, Dylan."

"Dylan?" She sounded excited rather than scared or angry.

That's a good sign.

She stepped into the bedroom and he reached over, turning on the nightstand lamp. She smiled, her eyes widening at the sight of his pecs. "Now this is a wonderful surprise." She paused. "How did you get in?"

"I bribed one of the staff. Don't tell."

She headed for the bed, stripping out of her workout wear, when she stopped. She glanced toward the bathroom, the shower still running, steam pouring through the door. "Is that for me?"

"I was told you were in the gym."

She smiled, holding up a finger. "Don't you dare move. I've got plans for you that will last all night."

He reached under the duvet. "*We're* looking forward to it."

She hopped once with excitement then rushed into the bathroom, humming happily at what was to come.

And the moment she hit the shower, he put his shirt back on and left, though not before leaving a quick note.

I'm sorry, darling, but work called. Another time, I promise.

Operations Center 3, CIA Headquarters

Langley, Virginia

Leroux stood in the state-of-the-art operations center, thankful to be out of the cramped confines of Kane's off-the-books equivalent. Though he did regret having to send Tommy Granger home, making the operation completely official was the right move, and one Morrison had agreed to the moment they had Natasha Ivashin in custody.

Now they were dealing government to government, though still through back channels. Natasha had been apprehended by West's daughter in Germany. Bringing the Germans into things could mean bringing the European Union in, possibly NATO, and too many other players.

And that meant questions.

Through Zorkin, a handover had been arranged, and an explanation for everything given that identified the players involved on the Russian side of things, protecting West and Morrison from being associated with the plot. The Russians appeared eager to avoid the plot going public, and to pin everything on Natasha and her accomplice, Minkin. How they would spin that, he didn't know, but it at least got Natasha out of their hands, as she had refused to cooperate, and Morrison had ordered she wasn't to be tortured, even if approved protocols were followed.

Regardless of her refusal to talk, they were all convinced she knew little to nothing. Everything, they were certain, had been provided to her by her uncle, a man whom they now had the identity of, and knew had the connections and means to provide her with the information and assets necessary to achieve her goal. She was protecting him, or at least trying to, by saying nothing.

It's already too late for him.

The deal was that once she was handed over, American representatives would be allowed to interrogate Cheslav Aristov to determine if there was any further threat, and to identify the final member of the conspiracy in 1988.

"We have confirmation. Cheslav Aristov has been arrested and is being transported to the agreed upon location."

Leroux acknowledged the update from Sonya with a nod.

"I'm kinda surprised they've agreed to this."

Leroux glanced at their whiz kid, Randy Child, as he spun in his chair, staring at the ceiling. "Why's that?"

Child shrugged. "Well, they're Russian."

Leroux chuckled, the reasoning sound. "Frankly, I'm surprised too, but I think they want the answers as desperately as we do, and they want us to back them up when we pin everything on Natasha and her so-called uncle. This whole nerve agent thing has embarrassed them on the world stage, and there's already talk of further sanctions. If they can clear themselves of this, and convince the world it wasn't a state sanctioned attack, I think they'd agree to anything short of sending a clean team to the next Olympics."

Laughter erupted from the room, the frivolity interrupted by another update from Sonya. "The rendition flight is landing now."

"That's another thing I'm stunned worked."

Leroux regarded Child. "You're in a pessimistic mood today."

Child shrugged. "Am I?"

"He broke up with his girlfriend."

Leroux frowned at the personal tidbit shared by someone in the back of the room. "Sorry to hear that. It happens. Are you good to work?"

Child's cheeks flushed from the embarrassment of his personal life being shared, his chair spinning brought to an abrupt end with the drop of a foot. "I'll live." He pointed at the screens, shifting the attention. "There she is."

Leroux turned to watch the coffin containing Natasha carried from the Aeroflot flight toward a waiting hearse. It was West's idea, something they had done before in the past, and still did to this day on occasion. Natasha had been wounded, though not fatally, West and his family treating her successfully while they awaited a CIA team's arrival for extraction. Once the agreement had been reached with the Russians, she was sedated with an IV drip that would keep her that way, placed in a pressurized coffin with an air supply, and loaded aboard a commercial cargo flight so as not to attract attention.

For the moment, everything was going as planned.

His eyes widened as he watched the satellite feed, another vehicle racing onto the tarmac. "What the hell's going on?"

Outside Ostafyevo International Business Airport

Moscow, Russia

Kane rested his elbows on the roof of the car, watching the unfolding scene through binoculars, an unexpected arrival rushing toward the handover of Natasha Ivashin. "This can't be good."

Zorkin nodded. "I told you I didn't trust them."

Kane stole a glance at the old man. "But you arranged it."

"I made the agreement with the Russian government. I wouldn't trust them to stick with any deal, but I don't think that's what's going on here. Watch."

Kane pressed his eyes back against the binoculars as gunfire erupted, the new arrivals slaughtering the team waiting for the coffin, then he smiled slightly as they emptied their magazines into the coffin. "You called it."

"We made a deal with the Russian government, but it's so corrupt, you can be sure that someone will always let the secrets slip for the right price."

Kane watched one of them with a portable circular saw rounding the coffin, making quick work of the hardware holding the lid in place, then the reaction to what they found inside. Something was tossed in the coffin by a frustrated assassin.

Kane squinted. "What was that?"

Zorkin leaned slightly closer with his binoculars. "I can't tell. A photo?"

"That's what I thought." He pursed his lips as the attackers raced off. They had only minutes before the authorities would be crawling all over the scene. Kane jumped in their vehicle. "I'll be right back."

Zorkin stepped away, shaking his head. "You're gonna get caught!"

But Kane ignored him. He hammered on the gas and raced down the road that lined the airfield, then blasted through the back gate left open by the assault team. He reached the isolated area of the airport reserved for the special Aeroflot flight, and brought the vehicle to a halt. He leaped out and sprinted over to the coffin, peering inside.

And smiled.

It was a photo of Natasha, from perhaps a few years ago, obviously provided to identify the target.

A target made up of 120 pounds of weights, with one 8½x11 piece of paper with a happy face drawn on it, no doubt by a cheeky Alex West.

Thank God for Zorkin's suspicious nature.

He hurried back to the car and climbed in, holding up the photo to his backseat passenger. "Recognize yourself?"

Natasha glared at him, ignoring it. "You should have let me die. I won't tell you anything."

Kane tossed the photo on the passenger seat and turned them around, heading back to the gate, the sleepy airport security finally sending a lone vehicle out to investigate what had just happened. Within minutes, Zorkin was occupying the passenger seat, examining the photo.

His eyes narrowed. "An interesting photo choice, don't you think?" He held it up for Kane to see.

Kane eyed it for a moment. He hadn't really noticed earlier in the rush of collecting it, but it wasn't a frame capture from a surveillance camera, but instead a photo of her standing in front of a home with a slight yet forced smile, her arm around a short, old woman with a beaming smile. "Not exactly a mugshot, is it?" He pursed his lips. "Show her."

Zorkin turned in his seat, holding up the photo for Natasha, the woman delivered in the same manner as described, but two hours earlier, the "body" picked up by her grieving brother and grandfather. "Recognize this photo? That's you and your mother, isn't it?"

Natasha glared ahead, saying nothing as Kane watched her reaction in the rearview mirror.

Then her eyes darted toward the photo, then her entire head turned as her mouth opened slightly.

"It is, isn't it?"

She nodded slowly. "Wh-where did you get this?"

Kane replied. "You saw me get it yourself. Those men who pumped a couple of pounds of lead into your coffin left it. It was supposed to be used to identify your body when they were done."

She slowly shook her head. "But that's impossible."

Kane tensed with anticipation as he suspected a revelation was about to be heard. "Why?"

She tore her eyes away from the photo. "Because that photo is on my uncle's desk, and there's only one copy." Her jaw dropped. "Did Uncle Cheslav just try to kill me?"

Kane took a deep breath as he guided them away from the scene, everything from the past three weeks being rewritten.

Minkin Holdings Safe House

Outside Smolensk, Russia

"Sir, we've got activity at the road. A vehicle is approaching."

Minkin smacked Svetlana on the ass and she crawled out of his lap, plopping onto the couch and grabbing a fashion magazine, one she used to grace the covers of before she had become "his." "Any idea who it is?"

"Not yet, but they're not just turning around. They're still approaching."

Minkin headed for the security office rather than speak to his team through the panels wired throughout the house. He stepped inside, frowning at the displays showing an SUV slowly approaching. He gestured at the screen. "If you were here for a hit, would you drive that slow?"

His head of security, Sergei, shook his head. "No, unless I wanted to look innocent."

"And would you send just one vehicle?"

"Yes, if I wanted to cause a distraction. I'd send the rest of my men through the woods surrounding the house."

Minkin tensed, checking the other cameras. "Are we showing anyone approaching?"

Sergei shook his head. "No, just some wildlife. Nothing human."

Minkin chewed his cheek. "Could they just be lost? Looking for directions?"

"Do you want to risk it?"

"We can't just kill them without knowing."

Sergei glanced over his shoulder at him. "If we go out there and challenge them without weapons, we could be killed. If we challenge them *with* weapons, and they're just lost tourists, they're going to report it, and we're not ready to get you across the border until tomorrow."

Minkin sighed, tapping his chin. Then smiled. "Svetlana!"

Kane stepped out of the vehicle, his arms held high, then opened the rear door, helping the handcuffed Natasha out. He leaned in, looking at Zorkin. "You coming?"

Zorkin frowned then turned off the engine. "Fine, but if I get killed, I'm going to be pissed."

Kane chuckled, always enjoying Zorkin's company. The man had been extremely well trained by the Soviets back in the day. His English was perfect, his idioms were spot on, and anyone would be hard-pressed to prove he wasn't a red-blooded American.

The three of them walked to within fifty feet of the front entrance to the impressive cabin tucked away in the forest outside Smolensk, a place no one would think to look for Minkin, a place Kane was certain was completely off-the-books.

A place now hosting Svetlana's luggage.

The door opened slightly, the owner of said luggage appearing, trembling with fear and the blast of cold. "Hello?"

"Ms. Lobanov. How are you?"

She brightened as she recognized him. "Mr. Insurance Man! What are you doing here?"

"I need to speak with Mr. Minkin. It's rather urgent. May we come in?"

She beckoned them to approach when she was pulled back inside by someone, a man Kane recognized from his brief meeting with Minkin appearing, pistol in hand.

"That's far enough."

They stopped, and Kane continued to do the talking. "My name is Dylan Kane. I'm here to speak to Mr. Minkin. We are all unarmed. I think Mr. Minkin will want to hear what I have to say." He pointed to Natasha. "Do you recognize her?"

The man stared at her for a moment then his eyes flared. "Yes!" He aimed his weapon at her. "You dare bring her here?"

"I think your employer will want to hear what she has to say as well." Kane took one step closer, the weapon redirected at him. "This will only take a few minutes, then you'll never see us again."

"Let them in."

The voice came from inside, and Kane recognized it as Minkin's. He took Natasha by the arm, Zorkin holding the other, and the three stepped inside, a significant security detail spread around the room, guns on display. Svetlana was curled up on a couch while Minkin took a seat near the fire. He didn't offer for them to sit.

"Mr. Minkin, it's good to see you again."

Minkin frowned. "How did you find me?"

Kane decided getting Svetlana in trouble wasn't in anyone's best interest, and besides, if the tracking devices planted on the luggage went undetected, it might prove useful should they need to find Minkin again. "We have very resourceful people at Langley."

Minkin grunted. "Let's just hope the Russian authorities aren't so resourceful."

"Let's."

Minkin folded his arms. "So, why are you here?"

Kane pulled out his phone and brought up a picture of Natasha's father with her uncle. "Do you recognize anyone in this photo?"

Minkin stared at the photo for a moment then his eyebrows rose. "Yes!"

Kane's heart rate picked up slightly. "And was he the man in charge?"

"Yes. I saw them together in the hallway after, and it was pretty clear who was in charge between the two of them."

Kane and Zorkin, and even Natasha, all stared at each other. Kane stepped closer, holding up the phone with the photo. "You're saying *both* these men were in the room?"

Minkin nodded. "Yes."

"You're sure?"

"Of course I'm sure. I was sitting at the head of the table. Remember, they wanted it to look like I was in charge."

"Which one briefed you?"

"The one on the left."

"That's my father," said Natasha, her voice barely a whisper, her eyes still wide with the shock of what had just been said. "W-was he in charge?"

Minkin shook his head. "No, the other one was."

"My uncle."

Minkin's jaw dropped as he grabbed the phone from Kane, zooming in on the second man. "*That's* your uncle?" He fell back in his chair, staring at the photo. "I didn't recognize him." He shook his head, his mouth agape. "I can't believe it. Cheslav Aristov was in charge of the entire operation!"

Kane took his phone back. "How can you be sure?"

"I saw them in the hallway afterward having a conversation. It was very clear who among the two was in charge."

Natasha dropped into a chair, her head shaking. "It can't be. Why would he lie to me about that? Why would he say he didn't know? Why would he say it was my father who told him everything?" She looked up at Kane. "Is that why he tried to have me killed today?"

Svetlana gasped. "Your own uncle tried to kill you? How horrible!"

Natasha's shoulders squared. "He's not my uncle. He's just my father's friend."

Kane frowned. "I think he was also your father's commanding officer." He sat beside her. "I think your uncle recruited your father because they were friends, and he knew he could trust him. Together, they recruited Mr. Minkin here to be the patsy should something go wrong."

Minkin grunted. "Which it did. I was ordered to clean everything up, so I'd be the one who took the fall if I was discovered."

"The others were probably on file as agitators against the state, disgruntled agents who didn't agree with the new reform policies."

"God knows there were enough of those," said Zorkin, the last to sit.

Minkin shrugged. "I was one of them. I thought we were making a big mistake, but, well, things worked out in the end."

Zorkin regarded him. "For you."

Again, Minkin shrugged. "I'm not going to apologize for my success. They were different times, and everyone was struggling to survive. I had some good dirt on a lot of the new leadership. No one was clean back then. I leveraged it into some good defense contracts, and the rest is history. At least our people aren't dying by the millions anymore."

Kane waved his hand, ending the tangent. "That means we now know all six people in the room."

Minkin eyed him. "*You* do. I still don't know who the American was."

"Nor will you. But everyone is now accounted for, and with Aristov now in custody, this is over."

Minkin grunted. "I wouldn't count on it. That man has resources, connections, money, and dirt on everyone. Now that I know who he really is…" He sighed. "A man like that is never in custody until he's dead. And even then, I'd want to see the body and shoot it a few times just to make sure." He wagged a finger, leaning back in his chair. "That man has ambitions. Why would he get himself elected now, at his age? Ego. He thinks he can do better than those leading us, which I don't think is much of a stretch. He wants power."

Kane eyed him. "I think *that's* the stretch."

"Is it? Look what he's done. He's had her running all over the place killing people in extravagant ways. Why Novichok? It can *only* be traced back to the Russian government, and embarrasses us on the world stage. Why a truck bomb? To make it look like Islamic extremists, so that the government looks weak on terror. Why a machine gun out of the side of a helicopter? To make it look like it was a grand conspiracy." He turned to Natasha. "He's been using you the entire time, my dear. He let you clean up his mess from thirty years ago, while making the government he wanted to challenge appear weak. If word had ever gotten out that he was involved in trying to assassinate Gorbachev, he'd be finished. And when you came to him, asking questions, he realized that what had been buried for so long was still a threat to him, so he figured out a way to use you, and you fell for it because you were so hellbent on revenge." He leaned forward. "I bet you he didn't agree to help you right away, did he?"

Natasha stared at him blankly. "No. He came to see me the next day."

"Exactly! He needed time to figure out what to do, and once he had figured out how to use you and the situation to his advantage, he agreed to help you on your little revenge quest."

"He never loved me." Natasha's voice cracked and her shoulders shook. Then she suddenly drew in a deep breath, her jaw squaring as she glared out at the world. "I want him dead."

Kane regarded her for a moment, an idea formulating. "Do you want to confront him?"

"With a gun."

Kane smiled. "I doubt that's possible. I mean a face-to-face. You can ask him anything you want, get some closure. You're going to prison for the rest of your life. There's no avoiding that. But at least you could serve your time with your questions answered."

She stared at him for a moment then nodded. "I'd like that."

Butyrka Prison

Moscow, Russia

"Natasha, what are you doing here?"

"Uncle" Cheslav Aristov leaped to his feet, rounding the table, his arms outstretched as one would expect any caring relative to do. But Natasha took a step back, shaking her head.

"Don't touch me."

He came to an abrupt halt, his eyes narrowing. "Why? What's wrong?"

"You lied to me."

Aristov bristled at the accusation, quickly regaining his composure. "That's a horrible thing to say to your uncle."

"You're not my uncle."

Her heart ached at the pain on his face, pain that from all outward appearances seemed genuine. She wanted to immediately apologize, but she knew the truth.

She just needed to hear it from his mouth.

She held up the photo the American had found at the scene of what was to be her execution. "Can you explain this?"

Aristov's eyes widened and his face paled before he finally sighed and dropped into the chair of the interrogation room she had been granted access to for ten minutes. Ten minutes to pry loose thirty years of lies. "What do you know?"

"Almost everything, but I want to hear it from you. I want the truth." She sat across from him, leaning in and peering up at his sunken face. "Tell me the truth, Uncle. I deserve as much."

He lifted his head and stared at her, the hurt in his eyes from the face that had helped raise her for most of her life threatening her resolve. "Very well. What do you want to know?"

"Who was in charge?"

"I was."

Her stomach flipped with the confirmation. "And you recruited Father?"

"Yes."

"Why?"

"We were best friends for years. I outranked him only because of my family's connections. I trusted him with my life, and we both recognized that Gorbachev's reforms were dangerous. We feared what might happen should the system fail, and we were trying to prevent that. It wasn't that we felt communism was necessarily the best way, it was stability we were trying to preserve. Gorbachev was moving far too fast, and things were quickly spiraling out of control. We felt that by removing him, we could slow things down and bring about reform in a more controlled manner."

"So, *you* were going to take over?"

Aristov chuckled. "No, my dear, I wasn't. I had no ambitions like that at the time."

"But you do now?"

He regarded her in silence, then finally answered. "I do." He gestured at the room. "Or at least I did."

"But not back then."

"No."

"Then who would have taken over?"

"It didn't matter. It would have been a hardliner, and the reforms would have been halted. But the people had already shown they wanted reform, so things would have continued after a while, but at a much slower pace."

She folded her arms, staring at him. "And my father felt the same way?"

"He did."

"And was anyone else involved beyond the six of you in the room?"

He shook his head. "No. Nobody knew. Our plan wasn't even to take credit. We would clean up anything that needed cleaning up after the fact, and let the system take care of the public aftermath with the framing of the Americans."

"Why didn't you kill everyone then? Why wait?"

"It would have raised too many questions, for one. The disappearance of a lowly agent, the one Boykov killed, was enough trouble. Then Minkin's decision to check Boykov into a hospital rather than kill him, caused more problems. If we had eliminated Minkin, and the American Agent West, people would have started to ask questions."

"You took a big risk letting them all live."

"That was your father's doing, in part. He convinced me it wasn't necessary, and he was right. The American disappeared after the Cold War, Minkin became so successful he'd never risk anyone knowing he was involved, Boykov lost himself in the bottom of a bottle so no one would believe him anyway, and then there was your father and me."

"What about Kulick and his partner?"

"I destroyed Kulick's career with a phone call, and the American Morrison was never a problem."

She regarded him for a moment, deciding if he was telling her the truth. It all made sense, but there was something missing, something her enraged emotional mind couldn't put a finger on. "You found everyone quite easily."

"Because I've kept track of them all over the years, just in case."

She bit her lip. "You used me."

His eyes narrowed. "What do you mean?"

"Your plan. It was so convoluted. So unnecessarily difficult."

He crossed his arms, leaning back in his chair. "What do you mean?"

"Nerve agents. Bombings. Helicopters. Sniper rifles. Why? You had the means all along to kill them all. Why have me use these methods?"

"I told you, to confuse them. With that American on the ground now a Director at the CIA, I had to assume he might know more than he should. By having you use the Novichok, I gave you access to kill Minkin, and I had everyone thinking the government was behind the attack in England, and not you. I was trying to help."

She shook her head. "No, you were trying to help yourself. Some people I've met explained it to me, their theory at least. And you already admitted enough for me to know they were right."

"What are you talking about?"

"You said your ambitions now included power. You were trying to destabilize the government in the hopes of taking over."

He shifted in his seat. "Nonsense."

"Everything you do is for your benefit. You used me to clean up your mess from back then, and you used me to try and gain power today." She shoved the photo across the table, a photo she had only ever seen on her uncle's desk, a photo that had always brought a smile to her face when she visited him. "And you tried to kill me."

His eyes filled with tears, but none escaped. Nor did any words of defense.

"I can't believe you would do that. You would kill me, the closest thing you have to a daughter, just to protect yourself? What kind of pathetic man are you?"

A tear finally did escape. "One who lost his way long ago, my child."

She stared at him, her fingers tracing the outline of the buckle on the belt the American had given her before the meeting had been arranged, the Russians relieved to find out she was still alive, so they'd have someone to parade in front of the cameras for the international press. "What do you mean?"

He stared at her, the tears flowing freely now, her resolve weakening. "I've carried a terrible burden all these years, one that I must tell you before I go to my grave."

Her chest tightened and her stomach churned. "What?" She gripped the belt buckle. "It involves Father, doesn't it?"

He nodded. "I lied to you."

"About what?"

He sighed, his shoulders slumping. "About everything."

Her heart hammered. "What do you mean?"

"I told you I was in charge, and I was. That's true. But your father didn't want any part of it. I convinced him to take part. I practically had to force him. He hated me for that, and it ended our friendship after the operation failed."

Her chest swelled with pride at the revelation her father wasn't a monster like the creature that sat before her. He was a good man, a man who wouldn't willingly take part in something so evil. She eyed her uncle. "If it ended your friendship, then why have you been so involved in my life all these years?" She gasped as the missing piece, the piece she hadn't been able to figure out, suddenly slid into place. "If *you* were in charge, then why did he kill himself? Why did he fear for us if the only other person who knew was you?"

Aristov's shoulders heaved as tears erupted anew. "I'm so sorry, little one, I didn't mean for it to happen, but I couldn't help it."

Natasha rose slowly from her chair. "What did you do? Tell me!"

He stared up at her with bloodshot eyes, his cheeks stained, his nose running. "I'm so sorry, little one, I didn't mean for any of it to happen."

"Tell me!"

"Your father, he didn't kill himself."

Her jaw dropped and she collapsed into her chair, gripping the arms. "Wh-what do you mean?"

"He didn't commit suicide. I-I killed him."

White hot rage engulfed her, her eyes flaring as she nearly tore the arms off the chair.

And he recognized the look, scrambling to find excuses for his inexcusable act. "It wasn't my fault. He was racked with guilt from the moment the operation failed. He felt we had betrayed our country, our profession, and dishonored ourselves. He felt guilty that the young officer, Dimitri Golov, had been executed, along with his American partner, for no reason. He wanted to come forward, to reveal the truth and face the consequences, no matter what they may be." He leaned forward, his hands clasped in front of him, pleading to her. "It would have destroyed us all! I was already positioning myself to take advantage of the fall, and if your father talked, it would mean either imprisonment in a labor camp for the rest of our lives, or death. We were both still reasonably young, we had so much of our lives left, but there was no reasoning with him. I had to do it! It was his fault, not mine! If he had only kept his mouth shut, he'd be alive today."

Through clenched teeth, she asked her final question. "So, you murdered him, then made it look like a suicide." He nodded. "His letter to me. It wasn't even written by him, was it?"

Aristov collapsed on the table. "No, I wrote it." He looked up at her. "I'm so sorry, little one."

"So am I." She pulled the two small blades hidden in the belt buckle and leaped forward, embedding them into her uncle's temples then twisted, killing him instantly before the guards could enter the room to stop her. She spun on them, raising her hands, but not dropping the daggers. "American, if you're listening, there's one thing you should know. My uncle is dead, but this isn't over. I put a contract on Morrison. It can't be stopped. I'm sorry."

Then she charged the guards, her arms swinging with the daggers, then gasped as her body was rocked with shot after shot, ending thirty years of misery swiftly and without mercy.

Just as she had always wanted, but never had the courage to do herself.

Operations Center 3, CIA Headquarters

Langley, Virginia

"What's his location?"

Leroux spun toward Sonya, snapping his fingers, her reply to Kane's question immediate.

"He's heading home. I'm contacting his security detail now."

Leroux glanced at Child, pointing at the screen without saying anything, his well-trained team knowing exactly what he needed, no time wasted with verbal communication. A map appeared of the area, a red dot showing Director Morrison's car, several camera shots appearing moments later showing his mini-motorcade consisting of his vehicle and two escort vehicles.

"I've got them, Dylan. Everything looks good. What's going on?"

"Natasha just killed her uncle, and before she was shot by security, she said that she put a contract out on the Chief that can't be stopped."

Leroux cursed, stepping closer to the displays. "So, payment has already been made or arranged, and there's no communication with the team."

"That's my interpretation. We need to get him secured and fast."

Leroux watched as the motorcade came to a stop at a red light. He turned to Sonya. "What's going on? Why aren't they going through?"

She shook her head, slamming a fist into her console. "I can't reach them."

He spun toward Child. "Check for any type of jamming in the area."

Child attacked his keyboard then pointed at the screen. "There's a cellular dead zone right where the Chief is. Somebody's jamming the signals."

"But we don't use cellular with our teams."

Child shook his head. "They're probably jamming everything, not just cellular. It's just that it's the easiest for me to detect. By the time I figure it out—"

Kane interrupted. "It'll be too late." He cursed. "We have to get a warning to them. Wait. Where's Sherrie and Fang? I thought they were supposed to be watching him too."

Leroux frowned. "Morrison relieved them once everyone was in custody. Nobody knew about the contract."

Child pointed at the screen then hammered at his keyboard. "I've got an idea!"

"What?"

"No time to explain."

Leroux turned to the screen, the light changing green, the motorcade advancing through the intersection when Child threw up his arms in victory.

"Done!"

Downtown Langley, Virginia

Morrison sat in the back of his chauffeured car, his eyes closed as he tried to relieve the burn. It had been a hectic week, and he thanked God every day of it that he had people like Kane and Leroux that he could rely upon. With those behind the attacks identified and in custody, the threat was over, and he could now rest easy and only worry about the dozens of other threats to his life that came in daily.

I can't wait to see Cheryl.

He had told his wife to stay at her sister's until things were settled and was looking forward to her return.

In fact…

He fished his cellphone out and dialed her number. He frowned at the lack of a signal.

That's odd.

"Sir, you should see this."

Morrison leaned forward between the seats to see what his driver, Tony, was pointing at, and his eyes widened at the sight of a video billboard with a flashing message.

WA42 CODE RED ALPHA.

He cursed. "We're about to be hit."

"Buckle up, sir."

Tony hammered on the gas, grabbing his mike as he did so. "Red Alpha, repeat, Red Alpha!" But there was no response. He tried again then tossed the mike aside in frustration. "We're being jammed, sir." He activated their lights and siren and accelerated, rushing past the lead vehicle, the other well-trained drivers picking up on the situation, both escort vehicles jumping into action. "Sir, Langley or your home?"

"Which is closer?"

"About the same."

"Langley."

Tony honked on the horn three times then cranked the wheel, hopping over the median as Morrison clicked his seatbelt in place. The escorts followed then suddenly Tony hammered on the brakes. "Get down!"

Sherrie White fished out her phone and swiped her thumb. "Hello?"

"Hey, Sherrie, it's Dylan. Please tell me you're close to the Chief."

"He stood us down as soon as you sealed the deal in Russia. Why?"

"There's a hit on him, and we can't reach his car."

Sherrie put the call on speaker so Fang, driving, could hear. "I'm with Fang right now. Where's the Chief?"

"Chris, send the tracking information to her phone."

"Right away."

Sherrie's phone vibrated and she tapped the message that popped up, a secure tracking application appearing showing their location and the Chief's, with a recommended route. "We're less than five minutes away."

"Are you armed?" asked Kane.

"Of course."

Fang leaned closer to the phone. "She's armed. It's a crime for me to be armed." She winked at Sherrie, patting the Glock tucked into her waist.

"Get there, see what—"

Leroux interrupted. "It's going down now!"

Sherrie cursed then shoved her phone in the dash mounted holder before climbing over the seat and into the back. Fang hammered on the gas, strategically using her horn and her advanced training to get them into the action before it was too late, while Sherrie accessed the trunk through the back seat, yanking the duffel bag carrying their small arsenal forward.

"Weapons check!"

Fang pulled her weapon and handed it back. Sherrie quickly made sure it was loaded then returned it. "You're good." Fang put it back in her belt before blindly holding out her hand. Sherrie slapped three magazines in it then checked her own sidearm before prepping the two MP5s.

I have a feeling we're going to need these.

"Three minutes!"

"Copy that!"

She clipped two flashbangs to her belt then pushed the MP5 submachine guns into the front seat before climbing back up front. She tapped her chest, the knock of her vest reassuring. "Sure am glad we're not very trusting."

Fang flashed her a grin. "You have *no* idea how excited I am right now."

Sherrie laughed. "I can see why Dylan likes you."

"He loves her! And if you get her killed, he's coming after you!"

They both laughed at Kane's voice through the phone then grew silent as evidence of what was happening ahead appeared. Cars traveling in the opposite direction were speeding, their drivers panicked, their passengers staring out the rear windows. Police sirens pierced the air, and hints of flashing lights ahead were visible.

"We're about to engage. Wish us luck."

"Be careful," replied Kane, the signal breaking up as if someone was jamming it. "And kick some ass for me."

Morrison sat in the back seat, hunched over as four men steadily approached, pouring heavy fire on the vehicle's windows, their weakest points, the bullet-resistant glass slowly splintering, their failure inevitable and imminent. His support teams were both pinned inside their vehicles by two more groups of four men doing the same, the occupants unable to even open their doors to engage.

They were all going to die, it was just a matter of time.

Unless you open your door.

They were here for him, not his security detail. If he allowed himself to be killed, they would leave, saving the nine men and women protecting him. His eyes burned as he thought of his wife and children, but they would understand. They knew his job, they knew the type of man he was, and they knew he could never stand by and let others die uselessly just to save his own life.

Their defeat was assured, and only he could prevent the slaughter that would ensue should the ballistic defenses of the escort vehicles fail first.

"I'm going out there."

Tony spun in his seat, staring back at him. "Are you nuts, sir?"

"It's the only way I can save your life and the others. They're here for me, not you."

"With all due respect, sir, we're here to protect you, and are willing to die to do that."

Morrison smiled at him. "And I appreciate and understand that, Tony, but not when the outcome is guaranteed. I'm not getting out of this. Support is too—"

The pattern of the gunfire changed briefly, and he poked his head up to see that two of their assailants had turned, redirecting their fire on an arriving local police car, the officers shredded the moment they arrived.

And it settled things in his mind.

"I'm going." He choked up at the words he was about to say. "Tell my wife and kids I love them, and that I'm sorry."

Tony stared at him, the man having served him for years, and clearly affected by the sacrifice about to be made. "Sir, you don't have to do this."

Morrison reached out and squeezed the man's shoulder. "Yes, I do."

He reached for the door and pulled the handle.

"Oh my God!"

Leroux wasn't sure who had cried out, but it didn't matter. They were all sharing that tortured soul's horror as they watched the assault unfold from various angles captured by traffic and security cameras. A dozen men were unloading on the three vehicles of the motorcade, the security detail trapped inside their vehicles, it only a matter of time before the windows failed and the deadly lead penetrated the interior, ending the lives of all involved.

"What's he doing?" cried Sonya, pointing at one of the images. Leroux's eyes shot wide and he rushed toward the displays as the rear door of Morrison's vehicle slowly opened.

He gasped as he realized what was happening, and his respect for the man grew beyond anything he could have imagined as he dropped to the floor, clasping his head in his hands. "He's sacrificing himself to save the others."

The room fell silent as everyone watched what was to be the end of the man who had affected so many of their careers, not the least of which was Leroux's. Morrison had recognized his abilities early on, had given him tougher and tougher assignments, then finally put him to the ultimate test with a honeypot trap that was Sherrie.

That one thing had changed his life, Sherrie falling in love with her target, the two of them now a couple with a real future.

All thanks to the man about to die on the screens in front of him.

He forced himself to look, to watch the murder, not out of morbid curiosity, but out of respect for the man who had changed his life so much, who had made him the man he was today by forcing him to take chances and go beyond his comfort zone.

His shoulders heaved as his chest ached.

Goodbye, sir.

Fang hammered on the brakes then threw open her door, taking the MP5 handed her by Sherrie and shoving the spare mags in her pocket. She quickly assessed the situation, her experience level far greater than her companion's, and cursed as she saw the door to the limousine open. She looked over the roof at Sherrie. "You take right, I'll take left. Shoot center of mass, keep advancing. Use the vehicles as cover. Got it?"

"Got it!"

"Take out the guys assaulting the lead vehicle, then advance. That should allow the security team to help. Execute in three, two, one, execute!"

Fang squeezed the trigger, single-shot selected, and the first assailant went down, then the second, Sherrie's weapon belching lead, her own targets dropping as they both rushed forward. The doors of the lead escort vehicle were thrown open as they charged past, the four members of the security detail pouring out. Fang took out two more on her side that were assaulting Morrison's vehicle, but the others on Sherrie's side had picked up on what was going on before they were taken out.

"Sherrie, look out!"

Sherrie hit the deck, her weapon going silent, as Fang redirected her fire, the security detail joining in, the two men shaking from the impacts of dozens of rounds as Fang switched to full-auto. Ahead, the four remaining assailants were already redirecting their fire and Fang took cover behind the hood of the limousine as two of the security detail, too slow to react, dropped behind her.

But the distraction was enough for the second detail to exit their vehicle and quickly end the siege. Fang rose slowly, her weapon still at the ready, carefully surveilling the area. "Check the targets!"

The detail quickly set upon the assailants, disarming them, even the dead, then handcuffing the few that were wounded but alive.

Sherrie approached the door, still half opened, her weapon aimed at the dead and dying. "Chief, are you okay?"

Morrison's voice, shaky but relieved, replied. "We're both good!"

Fang beamed a smile at Sherrie who turned toward the nearest set of traffic lights and gave a thumbs-up to the viewers at home.

Morrison Residence

River Oaks Drive, McLean, Virginia

Kane sipped his scotch, pleased his boss had remembered his penchant for Glen Breton Ice, a case now on hand at a home he had been welcomed into for the first time, though this wasn't the first time he had been here.

The first time, he had broken in and confronted Morrison on why he wanted one of his agents dead.

Namely him.

Aside from his family, the most important people in his life were gathered here, and thankfully, all were alive and happy. He had been forced to listen to the assault on a cellphone mounted in Fang's car, battling the edge of a jamming zone, that left him for several minutes thinking Sherrie was dead. Thankfully, his interpretation of what he was hearing was wrong.

He had watched the video of the assault after the fact, and was still impressed with the sacrifice Morrison was willing to make, and was thankful Fang and Sherrie had arrived in time to turn the tide of the battle. His level of respect for the man had always been high, but now that he knew he would die to save those under his command, it had reached an entirely new level. He raised his glass.

"To the Chief! I'm glad he's not dead!"

Everyone raised their glasses. "To the Chief!"

Morrison acknowledged the toast, then raised his own glass. "Thanks to you all, I'm here to tell the tale." He turned to Sherrie and Fang. "Especially my two angels."

Sherrie grinned. "Leif's Angels?"

Fang's eyes narrowed. "What's that?"

"You know, as in Charlie's Angels."

Kane laughed. "I guess that would make you Lucy Liu, hon."

Fang's eyes widened. "Ooh, I like her. Elementary is awesome."

Leroux raised his glass. "Agreed." He looked about. "Is your wife here, sir?"

Morrison nodded. "She's sequestered herself to the bedroom for the evening so I don't have to shoot her if she overhears anything."

Kane laughed. "Good thinking on her part."

Morrison turned to Kane. "There's one thing missing in your report that the Russians want an explanation for."

Kane glanced around the room. "Uh oh." He drained his drink and Leroux refilled it. "What's that?"

"Where did she get that belt from?"

Kane shrugged. "What belt?"

"The belt with the daggers embedded in the buckle, along with a listening device."

Kane smiled. "I'm sure I have no idea."

"Uh huh. Well, they're pissed. They're blaming us for taking away their opportunity to parade Natasha on the world stage to take the blame."

Kane grunted. "Well, that's odd. I thought she was shot to death, not stabbed."

Morrison eyed him. "In your world, I bet you think that makes sense."

Kane grinned. "Doesn't it?"

Morrison chuckled, draining his own drink. He held up the empty glass. "I think I like your taste in scotch, young man, but you make a terrible diplomat."

Kane raised his glass. "To being a terrible diplomat!"

A round of cheers went up, then Sherrie became serious. "So, what happens to Minkin?"

Morrison shook his head slowly as Leroux refilled his glass. "Nothing, unless the Russians track him down. He's disappeared, and with his money, I doubt he's resurfacing unless he wants to."

Leroux put the decanter back down. "He was used by Aristov. Was he really at fault for what happened in '88?"

"In '88, no, but today? Absolutely. He handed over the Novichok to save his own skin. If it weren't for him, Kulick and his daughter would never have been poisoned."

Leroux's head bobbed. "I guess you're right." He regarded Morrison. "I guess Minkin, West, and you are the only ones left that know anything about what happened."

Kane cleared his throat. "Well, we all know now."

Morrison smiled. "Let's just hope it's another thirty years before anyone cares."

Kane held up a finger. "Umm, we'll still all be alive then."

Morrison grinned. "I won't!"

Salisbury District Hospital

Salisbury, United Kingdom

DCI Nelson waved Hugh Reading over and leaned in, his voice low. “You can see him now. Five minutes.”

Reading patted his old colleague on the back. “You’re a good lad. Drinks later?”

Nelson smiled. “The boys and I will be there. It should be grand.”

“I’ve invited my son. He’s a copper now.”

“I heard. You must be proud.”

Reading’s chest swelled. “You have no idea. But if I’ve left this cursed earth and you ever hear of him considering joining Interpol, you smack him for me.”

Nelson laughed. “It’s a promise.” He became serious, pushing open the door. “Five minutes.”

Reading nodded then headed into the room containing the two remaining, and original, Novichok victims. Igor Kulick had just woken after weeks of slipping in and out of consciousness, and lay in bed appearing weak but on the mend, his daughter in the next bed, sleeping.

Kulick's eyes narrowed and fear crossed his face as Reading, an imposing figure, entered. "Who-who are you?"

"I'm Agent Reading from Interpol."

Kulick relaxed slightly and frowned. "Interpol? I don't think you guys have been at me yet. How many times do I have to answer the same things?"

Reading smiled and approached the bed, lowering his voice. "I have a message from Whiskey-Alpha-Four-Two."

Kulick's eyes widened as he drew a quick breath. "So, he got the message?"

Reading held up the piece of paper found in Kulick's wallet by Nurse Aldrin. Kulick slumped in the bed, the tension he must have been feeling since the moment he woke, eased. "He wants you to know that you and your daughter are safe now."

Kulick's shoulders heaved as his lips trembled, his eyes brimming with tears. He reached out and grabbed Reading by the arm. "Tell my old friend, thank you, and I hope one day to tell him some more Soviet jokes."

THE END

ACKNOWLEDGMENTS

The inspiration for this novel should be obvious to those who follow the news. The outrageous poisonings in Salisbury, carried out by the Russian government, were excellent fodder for a spy novel. But merely retelling events everyone had read about already, would be boring not only for you, the reader, but for myself, the writer. So, the idea of having the Russians innocent of the crime was born.

One thing many ask about writing is about the process used. I use both plotting and pantser methods, the former being a formal outline that I then write to, the other simply a "park your ass in front of the keyboard and write" method. Either way, both are a lot of fun, though pantsing it is a little more nerve-racking. And, regardless of the method used, I, like you, don't know the ending necessarily.

Like this novel.

I get as much pleasure in seeing how things work out as you do, and it's always fun to see all the threads come together in the end.

And a little side story concerning the Soviet joke about the hotel room eavesdropping. My favorite teacher growing up was my eighth and ninth-grade English teacher, Miss Boss. We were stationed in West Germany at the time, and some of the teachers went on a trip to Moscow. After returning, she told us the story about how they were briefed before going, given a long list of rules to obey, and to assume they were always being watched or listened to.

One day, the hotel room was a little chilly, so she said aloud as a joke that she wished it were warmer. When she returned later, it was. Now, was the KGB passing on guest complaints to the hotel staff? Probably not, but it is a fun little story.

As usual, there are people to thank. My dad for the research, Brent Richards for some weapons info, Susan "Miss Boss" Turnbull for her Soviet-era hotel story, the proofing and launch teams, and of course my wife, daughter, mother, and friends.

To those who have not already done so, please visit my website at www.jrobertkennedy.com then sign up for the Insider's Club to be notified of new book releases. Your email address will never be shared or sold, and you'll only receive the occasional email from me, as I don't have time to spam you!

Thank you once again for reading.

Made in the USA
Monee, IL
29 December 2022

23927375R00173